TRINIDAD NOIR

THE CLASSICS

TRINIDAD NOIR

THE CLASSICS

EDITED BY
EARL LOVELACE & ROBERT ANTONI

This collection is comprised of works of fiction. All names, characters, places, and incidents are the product of the authors' imaginations. Any resemblance to real events or persons, living or dead, is entirely coincidental.

Published by Akashic Books
©2017 Akashic Books

Series concept by Tim McLoughlin and Johnny Temple
Trinidad map by Sohrab Habibion

ISBN: 978-1-61775-435-7
Library of Congress Control Number: 2016953860

First printing

Grateful acknowledgment is made for permission to reprint the stories in this anthology. See page 254 for details.

Akashic Books
Brooklyn, New York
Twitter: @AkashicBooks
Facebook: AkashicBooks
E-mail: info@akashicbooks.com
Website: www.akashicbooks.com

ALSO IN THE AKASHIC NOIR SERIES

PARIS NOIR (FRANCE), edited by AURÉLIEN MASSON
PHILADELPHIA NOIR, edited by CARLIN ROMANO
PHOENIX NOIR, edited by PATRICK MILLIKIN
PITTSBURGH NOIR, edited by KATHLEEN GEORGE
PORTLAND NOIR, edited by KEVIN SAMPSELL
PRISON NOIR, edited by JOYCE CAROL OATES
PROVIDENCE NOIR, edited by ANN HOOD
QUEENS NOIR, edited by ROBERT KNIGHTLY
RICHMOND NOIR, edited by ANDREW BLOSSOM, BRIAN CASTLEBERRY & TOM DE HAVEN
RIO NOIR (BRAZIL), edited by TONY BELLOTTO
ROME NOIR (ITALY), edited by CHIARA STANGALINO & MAXIM JAKUBOWSKI
SAN DIEGO NOIR, edited by MARYELIZABETH HART
SAN FRANCISCO NOIR, edited by PETER MARAVELIS
SAN FRANCISCO NOIR 2: THE CLASSICS, edited by PETER MARAVELIS
SAN JUAN NOIR (PUERTO RICO), edited by MAYRA SANTOS-FEBRES
SEATTLE NOIR, edited by CURT COLBERT
SINGAPORE NOIR, edited by CHERYL LU-LIEN TAN
STATEN ISLAND NOIR, edited by PATRICIA SMITH
ST. LOUIS NOIR, edited by SCOTT PHILLIPS
STOCKHOLM NOIR (SWEDEN), edited by NATHAN LARSON & CARL-MICHAEL EDENBORG
ST. PETERSBURG NOIR (RUSSIA), edited by NATALIA SMIRNOVA & JULIA GOUMEN
TEHRAN NOIR (IRAN), edited by SALAR ABDOH
TEL AVIV NOIR (ISRAEL), edited by ETGAR KERET & ASSAF GAVRON
TORONTO NOIR (CANADA), edited by JANINE ARMIN & NATHANIEL G. MOORE
TRINIDAD NOIR (TRINIDAD & TOBAGO), edited by LISA ALLEN-AGOSTINI & JEANNE MASON
TWIN CITIES NOIR, edited by JULIE SCHAPER & STEVEN HORWITZ
USA NOIR, edited by JOHNNY TEMPLE
VENICE NOIR (ITALY), edited by MAXIM JAKUBOWSKI
WALL STREET NOIR, edited by PETER SPIEGELMAN
ZAGREB NOIR (CROATIA), edited by IVAN SRŠEN

FORTHCOMING

ACCRA NOIR (GHANA), edited by MERI NANA-AMA DANQUAH
ADDIS ABABA NOIR (ETHIOPIA), edited by MAAZA MENGISTE
AMSTERDAM NOIR (HOLLAND), edited by RENÉ APPEL & JOSH PACHTER
ATLANTA NOIR, edited by TAYARI JONES
BAGHDAD NOIR (IRAQ), edited by SAMUEL SHIMON
BERLIN NOIR (GERMANY), edited by THOMAS WOERTCHE
BOGOTÁ NOIR (COLOMBIA), edited by ANDREA MONTEJO
BUENOS AIRES NOIR (ARGENTINA), edited by ERNESTO MALLO
JERUSALEM NOIR, edited by DROR MISHANI
LAGOS NOIR (NIGERIA), edited by CHRIS ABANI
MARRAKECH NOIR (MOROCCO), edited by YASSIN ADNAN
MONTANA NOIR, edited by JAMES GRADY & KEIR GRAFF
MONTREAL NOIR (CANADA), edited by JOHN McFETRIDGE & JACQUES FILIPPI
NEW HAVEN NOIR, edited by AMY BLOOM
OAKLAND NOIR, edited by JERRY THOMPSON & EDDIE MULLER
PRAGUE NOIR (CZECH REPUBLIC), edited by PAVEL MANDYS
SANTA CRUZ NOIR, edited by SUSIE BRIGHT
SÃO PAULO NOIR (BRAZIL), edited by TONY BELLOTTO
SYDNEY NOIR (AUSTRALIA), edited by JOHN DALE

LONDON, UK

MOUNT PLEASANT,
TOBAGO

CARIBBEAN SEA

NORTH COAST
BLANCHISSEUSE
BLUE BASIN
SANTA CRUZ
VALLEY
NORTHERN
RANGE
CASCADE
WOODBROOK
PORT OF SPAIN ✪
LAVENTILLE
FOOTHILLS,
NORTHERN RANGE
CENTRAL
MARKET
CUNARIPO

SAN FERNANDO
MAYARO
MALGRÉTOUTE
NORTH TRACE

COLUMBUS CHANNEL

TRINIDAD

ATLANTIC OCEAN

TABLE OF CONTENTS

INTRODUCTION
REBELLION AND MEDIATION

O ur intention in *Trinidad Noir: The Classics* was first of all to highlight the work of writers from the twentieth century. Another initial intention was that we publish stand-alone short stories; this has not been faithfully adhered to, and there are two excerpts from longer works in the collection. Even the matter of who is a Trinidadian writer was up for debate, and while those presented in this volume are Trinidadian by birth, passport, or domicile, we seriously considered including others with less clear-cut credentials of citizenship.

As it turns out, *Trinidad Noir: The Classics* is a subversive offering, challenging the very categories we thought we had established for our guidance, expressing in its very shaping the tug of our different interests, ways of seeing, where we felt ourselves located, and the slipperiness of the concepts we were trying to define. What is classic? Who is Trinidadian? What is Trinidad noir? (By way of context, the original *Trinidad Noir* volume published by Akashic Books in 2008 and coedited by Lisa Allen-Agostini and Jeanne Mason comprised brand-new stories written in the twenty-first century.)

What we have done here is feature stories from writers who were largely part of the literary wave that swept in with Independence: V.S. Naipaul, Samuel Selvon, Harold Sonny Ladoo, Wayne Brown, Elizabeth Nunez, Robert Antoni, Lawrence Scott, Michael Anthony, Willi Chen, myself, and others. To these we have added C.L.R. James, the only presence from an earlier generation, as well as a new wave of younger writers, principally women. In addition we have included the poems "The Schooner *Flight*" from Derek Walcott—who is at least half Trinidadian—and "Homestead" from the too-long-ignored writer Eric Roach from our sister island of Tobago.

The result is a publication of many moods and themes that despite these compromises and perhaps because of them ends up being profoundly Trinidadian. The stories range from Robert Antoni's wildly comic "Hindsight" to the macabre landscape of Elizabeth Nunez's "Town of Tears." C.L.R. James's application of the myth of La Divina Pastora to the liberation of women can be contrasted with Shani Mootoo's lighthearted play on folklore in "The Bonnaire Silk Cotton Tree"; Michael Anthony's optimistic innocence in "The Valley of Cocoa" can be set against Lawrence Scott's "Malgré-toute"; and Ismith Khan's Uncle Zoltan, an intriguing con man, can be easily compared to the stoic character and the somber world of Harold Sonny Ladoo's quiet peasant, who in digging for water in the parched land is in fact digging his own grave.

These stories are all set in what looks like the last days of the colonial world. And while they are not all focused on crime (a common element of the noir genre), they direct attention to the violence of a society that has not quite settled accounts with the casualties of enslavement and indentureship.

One of the ways in which our literature has sought to restore to humanness those persons disadvantaged by colonial arrangements has been to highlight the heroic individual of the underclass. Joebell in my own story in this volume, who embarks on a quixotic journey to escape to America, is one such character. He shares the stage with a varied cast of other characters: V.S. Naipaul's Man-man; Algernon, the alert smart-man in Samuel Selvon's "The Cricket Match," endeavoring to fit himself into the flattering stereotype of the West Indian in colonial London; Ismith Khan's Uncle Zoltan, playing the same cool card of deception again and again; Assam, the Chinese shopkeeper in Willi Chen's story, outsmarting not only thieves but also the government; Wayne Brown's protagonist in "The Vagrant at the Gate"; and Ghost, the persuasive thief in Barbara Jenkins's "Ghost Story." None of these lead characters come across as obvious heroes; most evoke at least a degree of amusement, some pity, or, like Anansi the trickster, challenge us to understanding by showing us ourselves. Ghost, in Barbara Jenkins's story, is intriguing; although he moves like a ghost, he is still visible. We can still talk to him, whether in reprimand or consultation. We can pardon his violations of our space and his appropriation of our property because we know him.

In the rural seaside community where Jennifer Rahim's "Songster" is set, neighbors are still in touch with the good, the bad, and the ugly of their community. But when we come to the contemporary world portrayed in the stories of Elizabeth Nunez, Sharon Millar, and Elizabeth Walcott-Hackshaw, characters like Ghost have disappeared. The relationship with those at the margins of respectable society has shifted and crime becomes a dominant part of the landscape. Even so, these writers have not accepted the world as a place of violence, cruelty, and cynicism—as the noir genre might suggest. Instead, their characters view crime with genuine alarm and fear, as at an invasion they are powerless to repel. Indeed, crime is not a genre of fiction; it is a force that maims and kills and kidnaps. And while those who tell the stories are often onlookers rather than direct victims, what they feel is the enclosing darkness, physical and emotional, captured so well in "The Party" by Elizabeth Walcott-Hackshaw, whose protagonist is trapped in a world in which she must soldier on, keeping up appearances in a life endorsed by her actions but not embraced by her heart.

Trinidad itself is a relatively new society, one of the latest colonial settlements in the West Indies. What is remarkable about this place is that it contains influences from all parts of the globe: the Amerindian, the European, the African, the mulatto, the Indian, the Chinese, the Middle Eastern, and more—in all their fascinating combinations. At the same time, it is also a society established in colonial inequality and injustice, against which affected communities have continued to rebel.

Where this country is different even from its Caribbean sisters is the degree to which it has developed its folk arts—its carnival, its steel band, its music—as forms of both rebellion and mediation. These forms have not only continued to entertain us; they ritualize rebellion, speak out against oppression, and affirm the personhood of the downpressed. This rebellion is not evident with the same intensity as it used to be. Independence and political partisanship and the growing distance of the middle class from the folk, among other developments, have seen a fluctuation in the ideals of rebellion. Yet what is incontestable is that these arts have established and maintained a safe space for conflict to be resolved or at least expressed, not in a vacuum but in the face of a status quo utilizing its muscle and myths to maintain a narrative that upholds its interests.

As the situation becomes more complex and information more crucial, our literature is best placed to challenge or to consolidate these myths. Individually, we are left to decide on whose behalf our writing will be employed. In this situation, the struggle has been within the arts themselves—whether they see themselves as an extension of rebellion or art as entertainment. Although late on the scene and without the widespread appeal of the native and folk arts, our literature can lay claim to being part of these arts of rebellion, upholding and making visible the dismissed and ignored, lifting the marginalized into personhood, persuading us that a new world is required, and establishing this island as a place in which it can be imagined and created.

It is against this background that this fantastic anthology expresses and grapples with the questions of who we are, what is classic, who is Trinidadian, and what is noir.

Earl Lovelace
Port of Spain, Trinidad
February 2017

PART I

LEAVING COLONIALISM

LA DIVINA PASTORA

BY C.L.R. JAMES

North Trace

(Originally published in 1927)

O f my own belief in this story I shall say nothing. What I have done is to put it down as far as possible just as it was told to me, in my own style, but with no addition to or subtraction from the essential facts.

Anita Perez lived with her mother at Bande l'Est Road, just at the corner where North Trace joins the Main Road. She had one earthly aim. She considered it her duty to be married as quickly as possible, first because in that retired spot it marked the sweet perfection of a woman's existence, and secondly, because feminine youth and beauty, if they exist, fade early in the hard work on the cocoa plantations. Every morning of the week, Sunday excepted, she banded down her hair, and donned a skirt which reached to her knees, not with any pretensions to fashion but so that from seven till five she might pick cocoa, or cut cocoa, or dry cocoa or in some other way assist in the working of Mr. Kayle Smith's cocoa estate. She did this for thirty cents a day, and did it uncomplainingly, because her mother and father had done it before her, and had thriven on it. On Sundays she dressed herself in one of her few dresses, put on a little gold chain, her only ornament, and went to Mass. She had no thought of woman's rights, nor any Ibsenic theories of morality. All she knew was that it was her duty to get married, when, if she was lucky, this hard life in the cocoa would cease.

Every night for the past two years Sebastian Montagnio came down from his four-roomed mansion, half a mile up the trace, and spent about an hour, sometimes much more, with the Perez family. Always, he sat on a bench by the door, rolling cheap cigarettes and half-hiding himself in smoke. He was not fair to outward view but yet Anita loved him. Frequently half an hour would elapse without a word from either, she knitting or sewing steadily, Sebastian watching her contentedly and Mrs. Perez sitting on the ground just outside the door, smoking one of Sebastian's cigarettes and carrying on a ceaseless monologue in the local patois. Always when Sebastian left, the good woman rated Anita for not being kinder to him. Sebastian owned a few acres of cocoa and a large provision garden, and Mrs. Perez had an idea that Anita's marriage would mean relief from the cocoa-work, not only for Anita but also for her.

Anita herself said nothing. She was not the talking kind. At much expense and trouble, Sebastian sent her a greeting card each Christmas. On them were beautiful words which Anita spelt through so often that she got to know them by heart. Otherwise, nothing passed between the two. That he loved no one else she was sure. It was a great consolation; but did he love her? Or was it only because his home was dull and lonely, and theirs was just at the corner that he came down every night?

As the months slipped by, Anita anxiously watched her naturally pale face in the broken mirror. It was haggard and drawn with watching and waiting for Sebastian to speak. She was not young and her manner was not attractive. The gossiping neighbours looked upon her as Sebastian's property. Even in the cocoa-house dances (Sebastian never went because he did not dance) she was left to herself most of the time. And then, she loved him.

It came about that Anita's aunt, who lived at Siparia, paid her a surprise visit one Sunday. She had not visited North Trace for years, and might never come back again. Consequently there were many things to be talked about. Also the good lady wanted to know what Anita was doing for herself.

"And when will you be married, ma chère?" she asked, secure in the possession of three children and a husband. Anita, aching for a confidante, poured forth her simple troubles into the married lady's sympathetic ear. Mrs. Perez expatiated on Sebastian's wordly goods. Mrs. Reis, you remember, came from Siparia. "Pack your clothes at once, girl," she said, "you will have to miss this week in the cocoa. But don't mind, I know someone who can help you. And that is La Divina."

Of La Divina Pastora, the Siparia saint, many things can be written but here only this much need be said. It is a small image of some two feet in height which stands in the Roman Catholic Church at Siparia. To it go pilgrims from all parts of the island, at all times of the year: this one with an incurable malady, that one with a long succession of business misfortunes, the other with a private grudge against some fellow creature to be satisfied, some out of mere curiosity. Once a year there used to be a special festival, the Siparia fête, when, besides the worshippers, many hundreds of sight-seers and gamblers gathered at the little village, and for a week there were wild Bacchanalian carouses going on side by side with the religious celebrations. This has been modified but still the pilgrims go. To many, the saint is nothing more than a symbol of the divine. To more—like the Perez family—it possesses limitless powers of its own to help the importunate. From both parties it receives presents of all descriptions, money frequently, but ofttimes a gift from the suppliant—a gold ring, perhaps, or a brooch, or some other article of jewellery. Anita had no money; her aunt had to pay her passage. But she carried the little gold chain with her, the maiden's mite, for it was all that she had. It was not fête time, and quietly and by herself, with the quiet hum of the little country village in her ears, Anita placed the chain around the neck of the Saint and prayed— prayed for what perhaps every woman except Eve has prayed for, the love of the man she loved.

That Sunday night when Sebastian reached Madam Perez's house, the even tenor of his way sustained a rude shock. Anita was not there, she had gone to Siparia and was not coming back till next Sunday, by the last train. Wouldn't he come in and sit down? Sebastian came in and sat down on his old seat, near the door. Mrs. Perez sat outside commenting on the high price of shop goods generally, especially tobacco. But Sebastian did not answer; he was experiencing new sensations. He missed Anita's quiet face, her steady nimble fingers, her glance at him and then away, whenever he spoke. He felt ill at ease, somehow disturbed, troubled, and it is probable that he recognised the cause of his trouble. For when Anita landed at Princes' Town the next Sunday, Tony the cabman came up to her and said: "Sebastian told me to bring you up alone, Anita." And he had to say it again before she could understand. During the six-mile drive, Anita sat in a corner of the cab, awed and expectant. Faith she had, but for this she was not prepared. It was too sudden, as if the Saint had had nothing to do with it.

They met Sebastian walking slowly down the road to meet them. For an hour he had been standing by her house, and as soon as the first cab passed, started, in his impatience to meet her on the way. The cab stopped and he was courageous enough to help her down. The cabman jumped down to light one of his lamps and the two stood waiting hand in hand. As he drove off Sebastian turned to her. "Nita," he said shortening her name for the first time, "I missed you, Nita. God how I missed you!"

Anita was happy, very happy indeed. In her new-found happiness she came near to forgetting the Saint, whose answer had come so quickly. Sebastian himself was very little changed. Still he came every night, still Mrs. Perez smoked his cigarettes, ruminating now on her blissful future. But things were different. So different in fact that Sebastian proposed taking her to the little cocoa-house dance which was to come off in a day or two. It was the first time that they were going out together since that Sunday. Everybody who did not know before would know now, when they saw Sebastian taking her to a dance, a thing he had never done before. So she dressed herself up with great care in the blue muslin dress, and what with happiness and excitement looked more beautiful than she had ever seen herself. Then, as she cast another look in the mirror she missed something. "How I wish," she said with a genuine note of regret in her voice, "how I wish I had my little gold chain." Here, her mother, determined not to jeopardise her future, called sharply to her, and she came out, radiant.

The dance continued till long after five o'clock, but Anita had to leave at three. Sebastian got tired of sitting down in a corner of the room while she whisked around. He felt just a trifle sulky, for he had wanted to leave an hour before, but she, drinking of an intoxicating mixture of admiration, success and excitement, had implored him to stay a little longer. They went home almost in silence, he sleepy, she tired, each thinking the other offended. It was the first little cloud between them.

"It is nothing," thought Anita, "we shall make it up tomorrow night." She thought of something and smiled, but as she peeped at Sebastian and saw him peeping at her, she assumed a more serious expression. Tomorrow, not tonight.

Once inside the bedroom she started to undress quickly, took out a few pins and went to the table to put them down in the cigarette tin in which she kept her knick-knacks. Her mother, who was lying on the bed and listening with half-closed eyes to Anita's account of the dance, was startled by a sudden silence, followed by the sound of a heavy fall. She sprang down quickly, bent over the prostrate form of Anita, and turned to the little table to get the smelling-salts. Then she herself stood motionless, as if stricken, her senseless daughter lying unheeded on the floor. There, in its old place in the cigarette tin, lay a little chain of gold.

THE CRICKET MATCH

BY SAMUEL SELVON

London, UK

(Originally published in 1957)

The time when the West Indies cricket eleven come to England to show the Englishmen the finer points of the game, Algernon was working in a tyre factory down by Chiswick way, and he lambast them English fellars for so.

"That is the way to play the game," he tell them, as the series went on and West Indies making some big score and bowling out them English fellars for duck and thing, "you thought we didn't know how to play the game, eh? That is cricket, lovely cricket."

And all day he singing a calypso that he make up about the cricket matches that play, ending up by saying that in the world of sport, is to wait until the West Indies report.

Well in truth and in fact, the people in this country believe that everybody who come from the West Indies at least like the game even if they can't play it. But you could take it from me that it have some tests that don't like the game at all, and among them was Algernon. But he see a chance to give the Nordics tone and get all the gen on the matches and players, and come like an authority in the factory on cricket. In fact, the more they ask him the more convinced Algernon get that perhaps he have the talent of a Walcott in him only waiting for a chance to come out.

They have a portable radio hide away from the foreman and they listening to the score every day. And as the match going on you should hear Algernon: "Yes, lovely stroke," and "That should have been a six," and so on. Meanwhile, he picking up any round object that near to hand and making demonstration, showing them how Ramadhin does spin the ball.

"I bet you used to play a lot back home," the English fellars tell him.

"Who me?" Algernon say. "Man, cricket is breakfast and dinner where I come from. If you want to learn about the game you must go down there. I don't want to brag," he say, hanging his head a little, "but I used to live next door to Ramadhin, and we used to teach one another the fine points."

But what you think Algernon know about cricket in truth? The most he ever play was on the street, with a bat make from a coconut branch, a dry mango seed for ball, and a pitchoil tin for wicket. And that was when he was a boy, and one day he got lash with the mango seed and since that time he never play again.

But all day long in the factory, he and another West Indian fellar name Roy getting on as if they invent the game, and the more the West Indies eleven score, the more they getting on. At last a Englisher name Charles, who was living in the suburbs, say to Algernon one morning:

"You chaps from the West Indies are really fine cricketers. I was just wondering . . . I play for a side where I live, and the other day I mentioned you and Roy to our captain, and he said why don't you organize an eleven and come down our way one Saturday for a match? Of course," Charles went on earnestly, "we don't expect to be good enough for you, but still, it will be fun."

"Oh," Algernon say airily, "I don't know. I uses to play in first-class matches, and most of the boys I know accustom to a real good game with strong opposition. What kind of pitch you have?"

"The pitch is good," Charles say. "Real English turf."

Algernon start to hedge. He scratch his head. He say, "I don't know. What do you think about the idea, Roy?"

Roy decide to hem and leave Algernon to get them out of the mooch. He say, "I don't know, either. It sound like a good idea, though."

"See what you can do," Charles say, "and let me know this week."

Afterwards in the canteen having elevenses Roy tell Algernon: "You see what your big mouth get us into."

"My big mouth!" Algernon say. "Who it is say he bowl four top bats for duck one after the other in a match in Queen's Park oval in Port of Spain? Who it is say he score two hundred and fifty not out in a match against Jamaica?"

"Well to tell you the truth, Algernon," Roy say, now that they was down to brass tacks, "I ain't play cricket for a long time. In fact, I don't believe I could still play."

"Me too, boy," Algernon say. "I mean, up here in England you don't get a chance to practice or anything. I must be out of form."

They sit down there in the canteen cogitating on the problem.

"Anyway," Roy say, "it look as if we will have to hustle an eleven somehow. We can't back out of it now."

"I studying," Algernon say, scratching his head. "What about Eric, you think he will play?"

"You could ask him, he might. And what about Williams? And Wilky? And Heads? Those boys should know how to play."

"Yes, but look at trouble to get them! Wilky working night and he will want to sleep. Heads is a man you can't find when you want. And Williams—I ain't seen him for a long time, because he owe me a pound and he don't come my way these days."

"Still," Roy say, "we will have to manage to get a side together. If we back out of this now them English fellars will say we are only talkers. You better wait for me after work this evening, and we will go around by some of the boys and see what we could do."

That was the Monday, and the Wednesday night about twelve of the boys get together in Algernon room in Kensal Rise, and Algernon boiling water in the kettle and making tea while they discuss the situation.

"Algernon always have big mouth, and at last it land him in trouble."

"Cricket! I never play in my life!"

"I uses to play a little 'pass-out' in my days, but to go and play against a English side! Boy, them fellars like this game, and they could play, too!"

"One time I hit a ball and it went over a fence and break a lady window and . . ."

"All right, all right, ease up on the good old days, the problem is right now. I mean, we have to rally."

"Yes, and then when we go there everybody get bowl for duck, and when them fellars batting we can't get them out. Not me."

But in the end, after a lot of blague and argument, they agree that they would go and play.

"What about some practice?" Wilky say anxiously. Wilky was the only fellar who really serious about the game.

"Practice!" Roy say. "It ain't have time for that. I wonder

if I could still hold a bat?" And he get up and pick up a stick Algernon had in the corner and begin to make stance.

"Is not that way to hold a bat, stupid. Is so."

And there in Algernon room the boys begin to remember what they could of the game, and Wilky saying he ain't playing unless he is captain, and Eric saying he ain't playing unless he get pads because one time a cork ball nearly break his shin-bone, and a fellar name Chips pull a cricket cap from his back pocket and trying it on in front a mirror.

So everything was arranged in a half-hearted sort of way. When the great day come, Algernon had hopes that they might postpone the match, because only eight of the boys turn up, but the English captain say it was a shame for them to return without playing, that he would make his side eight, too.

Well that Saturday on the village green was a historic day. Whether cold feet take the English side because of the licks the West Indies eleven was sharing at Lord's I can't say, but the fact is that they had to bowl first and they only coming down with some nice hop-and-drop that the boys lashing for six and four.

When Algernon turn to bat he walk out like a veteran. He bend down and inspect the pitch closely and shake his head, as if he ain't too satisfied with the condition of it but had to put up with it. He put on gloves, stretch out his hands as if he about to shift a heavy tyre in the factory, and take up the most unorthodox stance them English fellars ever did see. Algernon legs wide apart as if he doing the split and he have the bat already swing over his shoulder although the bowler ain't bowl yet. The umpire making sign to him that he covering the wicket but Algernon do as if he can't see. He make up his mind that he rather go for l.b.w. than for the stumps to fly.

No doubt an ordinary ball thrown with ease would have had him out in two-twos, but as I was saying, it look as if the unusual play of the boys have the Englishers in a quandary, and the bowler come down with a nice hop-and-drop that a baby couldn't miss.

Algernon close his eyes and he make a swipe at the ball, and he swipe so hard that when the bat collide the ball went right out of the field and fall in the road.

Them Englishers never see a stroke like that in their lives. All heads turn up to the sky watching the ball going.

Algernon feel like a king: only thing, when he hit the ball the bat went after it and nearly knock down a English fellar who was fielding silly-mid-on-square-leg.

Well praise the lord, the score was then sixty-nine and one set of rain start to fall and stop the match.

Later on, entertaining the boys in the local pub, the Englishers asking all sorts of questions, like when they stand so and so and why they make such and such a stroke, and the boys talking as if cricket so common in the West Indies that the babies born either with a bat or a ball, depending on if it would be a good bowler or batsman.

"That was a wonderful shot," Charles tell Algernon grudgingly. Charles still had a feeling that the boys was only talkers, but so much controversy raging that he don't know what to say.

"If my bat didn't fly out of my hand," Algernon say, and wave his hand in the air dramatically, as if to say he would have lost the ball in the other county.

"Of course, we still have to see your bowling," the English captain say. "Pity about the rain—usual English weather, you know."

"Bowling!" Algernon echo, feeling as if he is a Walcott

and a Valentine roll into one. "Oh yes, we must come back some time and finish off the match."

"What about next Saturday?" the captain press, eager to see the boys in action again, not sure if he was dreaming about all them wild swipe and crazy stokes.

"Sure, I'll get the boys together," Algernon say.

Algernon say that, but it wasn't possible, because none of them wanted to go back after batting, frighten that they won't be able to bowl the Englishers out.

And Charles keep reminding Algernon all the time, but Algernon keep saying how the boys scatter about, some gone Birmingham to live, and others move and gone to work somewhere else, and he can't find them anywhere.

"Never mind," Algernon tell Charles, "next cricket season I will get a sharp eleven together and come down your way for another match. Now, if you want me to show you how I make that stroke . . ."

HOMESTEAD

BY ERIC ROACH

Mount Pleasant, Tobago
(Originally published in 1953)

Seven splendid cedars break the trades
from the thin gables of my house,
seven towers of song when the trades rage
through their full green season foliage.
but weathers veer, the drought returns,
the sun burns emerald to ochre
and thirsty winds strip the boughs bare,
then they are tragic stands of sticks
pitiful in pitiless noons
and wear dusk's buskin and the moon's.

And north beyond them lie the fields
which one man laboured his life's days,
one man wearying his bone
shaped them as monuments in stone,
hammered them with iron will
and a rugged earthy courage.
and going, left me heritage.
is labour lovely for a man
that drags him daily into earth
returns no fragrance of him forth?

The man is dead but I recall

him in my voluntary verse,
his life was unadorned as bread,
he reckoned weathers in his head
and wore their ages on his face
and felt their keenness to his bone
the sting of sun and whip of rain.
he read day's event from the dawn
and saw the quality of morning
through the sunset mask of evening.

In the fervour of my song
I hold him firm upon the fields
in many homely images.
His ghost's as tall as the tall trees;
he tramps these tracks his business made
by daily roundabout in boots
tougher and earthier than roots;
and every furrow of the earth
and every shaken grace of grass
knows him the spirit of the place.

He was a slave's son, peasant born,
paisan, paisano—those common
men about the field, world over,
of sugar, cotton, corn or clover
who are unsung but who remain
perpetual as the passing wind,
unkillable as the frail grass;
who, from their graves within their graves,
nourish the splendour of the earth
and give her substance, give her worth.

Poets and artists turn again,
construct your cunning tapestries
upon the ages of their acres,
the endless labours of their years;
still at the centre of their world
cultivate the first green graces,
courage, strength and kindliness,
love of man and beast and landscape;
still sow and graft the primal good,
green boughs of innocence to God.

THE VALLEY OF COCOA

BY MICHAEL ANTHONY

Mayaro

(Originally published in 1961)

There was not much in the valley of cocoa. Just the estate and our drying-houses, and our living-house. And the wriggling little river that passed through.

And, of course, the labourers. But they didn't ever seem to speak to anyone. Always they worked silently from sunrise to evening. Only Wills was different. He was friendly, and he knew lots of other things besides things about cocoa and drying-houses.

And he knew Port of Spain. He knew it inside out, he said. Every day after work he would sit down on the log with me and would tell of the wonderful place.

As he spoke his eyes would glow with longing. The longing to be in that world which he said was part of him. And sometimes I knew pain. For Wills had made the city grow in me, and I knew longing, too.

Never had I been out of the valley of cocoa. Father was only concerned about his plantation, and nothing else. He was dedicated to wealth and prosperity, and every year the cocoa yielded more and more. So he grew busier and busier, building, experimenting, planning for record returns. Everything needed out of the valley was handled by Wills—for people who knew Port of Spain could handle anything. Business progressed. The valley grew greener with cocoa, and the

drying-houses were so full that the woodmen were always fell-
ing timber to build more.

Wills, who one day had just returned from ordering new
machinery in Port of Spain, sat talking with me. The sun had
not long gone down but already it was dusk. Wills said it was
never so in Port of Spain. Port of Spain was always bright. He
said as soon as the sun went down the whole city was lit by
electric lamps, and you could hardly tell the difference between night and day. And he explained all about those lamps
which he said hung from poles, and from the houses that lined
the million streets.

It was thick night when we stopped talking and got up. In
the darkness Wills walked straight on to a tree, and he swore,
and said, By Jove—if that it could have happened to him in
Port of Spain! He said one of those days I'd go there, when
I got big, and I'd see for myself, and I'd never want to come
back to the valley again.

The machinery arrived soon afterwards. It came in a shining
new van, and the name of the company was spelt in large letters on the sides of the van. The driver was a bright-looking
man and when the van stopped he jumped out and laughed
and called, "Hey, there!"

Wills and Father went down to meet him and I eased up
behind them. I was thrilled. It was not every day that strangers
came to the valley.

Father looked worried as he spoke to the man about payments. He complained that business wasn't doing well and
the machinery was so expensive. But the man was laughing
all the time, and said who cared about payments when Father
had all the time in the world to pay. Father was puzzled, and
the man said, yes, Father could pay instalments. Wills said it

was true, that's what they did in Port of Spain. The man made Father sign up for instalments and while Father signed, the man pulled at my chin and said, "Hi!"

Father was paying the first instalment. The man stretched his hands for the money and without counting it he put it into his pocket. Every time my eyes caught his he winked.

"Hi!" he said softly.

I twined round Father's legs.

"Bashful," he said, "bashful," and he tugged at the seat of my pants. I couldn't help laughing.

He opened the door of the van and the next moment he was beside me. He was smiling and dangling a bright coloured packet. I held on to Father's legs. Then I felt something slide into my pocket. I looked up. "Like sweets?" the man said. I turned away and grinned.

From about my father's legs I watched him. He pulled out a red packet of cigarettes. He passed the cigarettes to Father, then to Wills, and as he lit theirs and lit himself one, he seemed to be taken up with the estate below.

"All yours?" he asked after a while.

Father nodded.

He shook his head approvingly. "Nice—nice, old man!"

The evening was beginning to darken and the man looked at his watch and said it was getting late and he'd better start burning the gas. Father said true, because Port of Spain was so far, and the country roads were bad enough. The man claimed there were worse roads in some parts of Port of Spain. He laughed and said, "What's a van anyway, only a lot of old iron." Father and Wills laughed heartily at this, while the man turned a silver key and started the van. Then he said, well cheerio, cheerio, and if anything went wrong with the machine he'd hear from us.

The days that followed were filled with dream. I continually saw the grand city, and the bright, laughing man. Port of Spain, I kept thinking. Port of Spain! I imagined myself among the tall, red houses, the maze of streets, the bright cars and the vans darting to and fro; the trams, the trains, the buses; the thousands of people everywhere. And always I heard the voice. "Hi!"—it kept sailing back to me. And every time I heard it I smiled.

Months passed, and more and more I grew fed up with the valley. I felt a certain resentment growing inside me. Resentment for everything around. For Father, for the silly labourers; even for Wills. For the cocoa trees. For the hills that imprisoned me night and day. I grew sullen and sick and miserable, tired of it all. I even wished for Father's fears to come true. *Witchbroom!* I wished witchbroom would come and destroy the cocoa and so chase Father from this dreary place.

As expected, the machinery soon went wrong. It wouldn't work. Wills had to rush to Port of Spain to get the man.

I waited anxiously towards the end of that evening, and when in the dusk I saw the van speeding between the trees I nearly jumped from sheer gladness.

From the hill Father shouted saying he didn't know what was wrong but the machine wouldn't start. The man said all right and he boyishly ran up to the hill to the house. He stopped and tugged at me and I twined round Father's legs. The man tickled me and we both laughed aloud. Then he gave me sweets in a blue and white packet, and he said he'd better go and see to the machine because the machine was lazy and didn't want to work.

He tried to tickle me again. I jumped away and we

laughed, and Father and Wills and he went to the shed. They had not been there five minutes when I heard the machine start again.

The labourers had changed a little. They had become somewhat fascinated by the new machine. It seemed they sometimes stole chances to operate it, for the machine went wrong quite a number of times afterwards. And so, happily, the man often came to us.

In time Father and he became great friends. He gave Father all the hints about cocoa prices in the city and about when to sell and who to sell to. He knew all the good dealers and all the scamps, he said.

He knew all the latest measures taken to fight cocoa diseases and he told Father what they did in West Africa, and what they did here and what they did there, to fight this, that, and the other disease.

With his help Father did better than ever. And he was so pleased that he asked the man to spend a Sunday with us.

"Sure!" the man agreed. And I ran out then, and made two happy somersaults on the grass.

That Sunday, when the man arrived, I was down the other side of the hill grazing the goats. The voice had boomed down towards me.

"Kenneth!"

I turned and looked round. Then I dropped the ropes and ran excitedly up the hill. "Coming!" I kept saying. "Coming!" When I got there the big arms swept me up and threw me up in the air and caught me.

Directly Father called us in to breakfast and afterwards the man put shorts on and we went out into the fresh air. The whole valley of cocoa nestled in the distance below us. The man watched like one under a spell.

"Beautiful!" he whispered, shaking his head. "Beautiful!"

"And the river," I said. Strange! I had hardly noticed how pretty the river was.

"Yes," the man answered. "Yellow, eh?"

I grinned.

"The water good?"

"Yes," I said.

"Sure, sure?"

"Sure, sure," I said.

"Well, come on!" He took me by the hand and we hastened into the house.

The next moment we were running down the hill towards the river, the man in bathing trunks and me with my pants in my hand and sun all over me. We reached the banks and I showed where the water was shallow and where it was deep, and the man plunged into the deep part. He came to the surface again, laughing and saying how nice the water was. He said there was no such river in Port of Spain. He told me to get on his back, and he swam upstream and down with me and then he put me down in the shallow part. Then he soaped my body and bathed me, and when I was rinsed we went and sat a little on the bank.

He sat looking around at the trees and up at the hill. I looked, too, at the view. The cocoa trees seemed greener than I ever remembered seeing them, and the immortelles which stood between the cocoa, for shade, were like great giants, their blooms reddening the sky.

I looked up at him. We smiled.

Quietly, then, he talked of the city. He told me the city was lovely, too, but in a different way. Not like it was here. He said I must see the city one of these days. Everything there was busy. The cars and buses flashed by, and people hurried into the shops, and out of the shops and everywhere. He said he liked the city. It had shops, stores, hotels, hospitals, post offices, schools—everything. Everything that made life easy. But sometimes he grew tired, he said, of the hustle and bustle and nowhere to turn for peace. He said he liked it here, quiet and nice. As life was meant to be. Then his eyes wandered off to the green cocoa again, and the immortelles, and here at the river, and up again to our house on the hill.

And he smiled sadly and said that he wished he was Father to be living here.

We went back into the water for some time. Afterwards the man dried my skin, and his, and we went up to the house.

After we had eaten, Father took us into the cocoa field.

It was quiet there between the trees. The dried brown leaves underfoot, together with the ripening cocoa, put a healthy fragrance in the air.

It was strange being so near those trees. Before I had only known they were there and had watched them from the house, but now I was right in the middle of them, and touching them.

We passed under immortelle trees. The ground beneath the trees was red with dropped flowers and the man picked up the loveliest of the flowers and gave them to me. Father broke a cocoa pod, and we sucked the seeds and juicy pulp, and really, the young cocoa was as sweet as Wills had told me. The man sucked his seeds dry and looked as if he wanted more, so I laughed. And Father, watching from the corner of his eyes, understood, and said, "Let's look for a nice ripe cocoa."

It was already evening when we took the path out. Father and the young man were talking and I heard Father ask him what he thought of the place.

"Great, Mr. Browne," he answered. "Mr. Browne, it's great, I'm telling you!"

Later, late that night, I eased up from the bed. I unlatched the window and quietly shifted the curtain from one side.

The valley lay quietly below. The cocoa leaves seemed to be playing with the moonlight and the immortelles stood there, looking tall and lonely and rapt in peace. From the shadows the moonlight spread right across the river and up the hill.

"Beautiful . . . !" the voice sailed back to my mind. And I wondered where he was now, if he was already in Port of Spain. He had been sorry to leave. He had said this was one of the happiest days he had known. I had heard him telling Father how he liked the valley so much and how much he liked the little boy. I had cried then.

And now it swept back to my mind—what he had told Father just as he was leaving. He had said, "Mr. Browne, don't be afraid for witchbroom. Not a thing will happen. Just you use that spray—you know—and everything will be all right."

Quickly then I drew the curtains and latched the window. And I squeezed the pillow to me, for joy.

PART II

FACING INDEPENDENCE

THE QUIET PEASANT

by Harold Sonny Ladoo

Tola

(Originally published in 1973)

Gobinah wasn't the kind of man to eat in the dark. He used to say that night is the time for a man to sleep and probe the meaning of his dreams; it is a time too for him to think about his crops and meditate on the future of his children; life isn't worth living if a man prefers to wake after the sun has travelled far in the sky; a man is supposed to wake before the sun and feel the sweat streaming out of his body, and the mud caking his feet and hands while there is still the mysterious darkness, for without this exposure and personal closeness to the primeval earth, it would be totally impossible for any man to enjoy good health.

It was March and the tomatoes he had planted in the ratoon caneland were dying off for water. March is always a terrible month for planting things in Carib Island, and most farmers in Lima, fearing the dryness of the earth, never bothered to plant a single seed during the dry season. Instead of trying to quarrel with the drought, the farmers in the area drank their rum, reaped their cane and looked after their animals. But Gobinah was different. Other men had their wives to help them in the fields, and their grown sons helped them with their cattle. Once Batulan had worked side by side with Gobinah. First it started as a little cough and Batulan drank bush medicine and consulted Bhola Saddhu, the village priest of Tola. Months later the D.M.O. in Tolaville said that Batulan had TB. Most men in Tola would have beaten their wife out of the village, but Gobinah didn't do this. He accepted her illness as his destiny and continued to work the soil. In order to pay medical bills he sold his crops and his cattle and never became depressed.

In the end he remained with the black double-jointed bull; he considered the animal his friend and he couldn't sell it. Some months ago a few wicked villagers had poisoned the animal. Most men in Tola would have gone on the warpath and killed somebody, but Gobinah believed in abstract justice, so he left the matter alone. Gobinah could have made some money, because butchers came to buy the dead animal to sell the meat in South City Market. Instead of selling the bull Gobinah dug a grave and buried it in the ratoon caneland. In the night the butchers came with lanterns and guns, dug out the carcass and carried it away.

Because he had no money to pay someone to cart his cane to the derrick, he cutlassed down most of the ratoon cane, dug up the earth with a fork and a hoe, and planted tomatoes. Sita, his eldest daughter, was already fifteen, and in May she would be married off to a crab-catcher in Jangli Tola. Although the crab-catcher belonged to the chamar caste (the lowest caste), he had demanded tilak (dowry). This dowry was important and Gobinah knew that only a madman would marry his daughter without it. His four other daughters were still too young to be of any real bother, and perhaps when they would come of age he wouldn't have to worry too much, because they were pupils at the Tolaville Mission School. Daily girls with a little education were getting jobs in the cities and looking after themselves. Perhaps Sita would have had her fair share of education, if Batulan hadn't contracted consumption.

With his whole mind centred on the work, and his powerful arms holding the fork, Gobinah continued digging the well. He had already crossed six feet, the earth became softer and colder, yet there were no signs of water. Long before daybreak he had started digging, but the top soil was hard like iron. Now, however, it was easier for him to dig. The earth felt cold under his feet and his skin became taut as the direct rays of the sun hit his body.

Raju, the ten-year-old son of Gobinah, was weeding the yard with an old hoe. As he was putting some dirt around the small zaboca tree Batulan came out of the kitchen. Holding her chest she coughed. The boy heard the racking inside her chest but he didn't look. Then Batulan spat out the phlegm and blood, saying, "Beta (son), time to carry some food for you bap (father) in the land."

"Ha (yes), Mai (mother)," he said, as he dropped the hoe on the ground. When he approached the drain he saw the chunks of blood that had come out of his mother's chest resting like small red flowers on the parched earth. When he reached inside the kitchen, Sita handed him a basket. Inside the basket, the roti and fried allou were wrapped in banana leaves. Then she put some rainwater into the bolee (calabash) and handed it to him. Without saying anything to his sister, the boy walked out of the house. He was going to meet his father in the caneland, and the land was a little over a mile away from the house. To get to his father he had to pass through the land of other farmers. Often the farmers cursed and swore at him, and many times they made their grown sons beat him with bamboo switches. To avoid the farmers he walked through the bamboo grass. Since he was barefooted and naked except for the short and torn khaki pants that were held up by the strand of corbeau liana tied around his waist, he felt the sun eating through his skin. Now he was near the two acres of land that his father rented from the whiteman. Thirsty, he drank some water from the bolee and looked up at the sky; it was blue, with hardly a strand of cloud anywhere. When he walked into the land he saw the tomatoes' leaves all crumpled up; the leaves were pale, but here and there he saw little gold spots, and he recognised them as the tiny flowers. As soon as he reached the mound of freshly dug earth, he called out, "Ay, bap!"

"Ha, beta," his father answered.

"I bring you food, bap."

"Send it down, beta."

Slowly, carefully, the boy walked on top of the fresh dirt. The well was deeper than ten feet now, and still there wasn't any sign of water in it. Wearing a soiled and torn dhoti (loincloth), bare-back and barefooted, he saw his father inside the hole. Sweat was flowing from every pore in his body; with the earth caking his hands and feet, the man asked, "How de tomatoes lookin, beta?"

As if expecting the whole plantation to change miraculously, the boy looked at the tomatoes again, before saying, "De garden lookin bad, bap."

The man said nothing. First the boy threw the basket down inside the well; the man caught it, took out the food and flung the basket back for his son. Next the boy sent down the water. Resting the water at his feet, opening the roti and allou, the man asked, "You go eat some food, beta?"

"No, bap, I done eat."

With his toes hidden in the earth, with his back resting against the cold earth, the man ate his food. Raju stood at the top looking down at his father. He noticed that the man's feet trembled now and then, and his hands shook as he brought the food to his mouth. His face, neck and chest were red and his veins stood out as thick as corbeau lianas. Dropping the banana leaves inside the well, drinking the water from the bolee, throwing the container up for his son, Gobinah said, "So de garden lookin bad, beta?"

"Ha, bap."

Gobinah shook his head. "Soon as I get worta in dis well, beta, everything goin to be oright. Wen I reap dis tomatoes I goin to pay de whiteman his rent. If I don't pay de rent, he goin to take away de land. Den I goin to give tilak for Sita to get married."

"Yeh, bap."

"Now, beta, you modder kinda sickly. A few days every week, try and go to school and learn someting. Take education, beta, so wen you come a man, you wouldn't have to kill youself for a bread like me." Wiping his brows with his soiled hands, he continued, "When you have education, beta, you wouldn't have de cause to rent land from dese white people. And wen you come a man, beta, try and make youself oright."

"Yeh, bap," Raju said sadly. Looking at his father, he said, "Well, bap, maybe you could take a rest now. Tomorrow you could dig some more."

"No, beta. I must get worta in dis hole today. Dem tomatoes deadin for worta. If dis crop dead off, beta, den de whiteman goin to take back de land, and de ten years dat I payin rent wouldn't stop him from takin it. Den dis crop have to make enuff money for you sista to get married. She is a big gal now, beta, and I cant keep she too long again in de house."

After the man talked some more, he took up the fork again and continued digging. Now the hole was too deep for him to swing the dirt up with the fork. He took up the dirt, made it into small balls, and flung them out of the hole.

"Lemme help you, bap."

"No, beta, de sun too hot. Go and siddown inside dem ratoon cane. Wen I get worta, I goin to call you."

"Oright, bap."

Exhausted by the heat of the sun Raju took the basket and bolee and walked to the ratoon cane. Then he thrashed some dry leaves and sat on them. From his hiding place he saw the little balls of dirt darting out of the well. As he waited for his father to call, he dozed off. Suddenly he woke with a start; during his sleep he had heard his father calling, just his eyes couldn't open at the time. Wiping his eyes with the back of his hands, he noticed that it was almost evening; he noticed too that no small balls of earth came flying out of the hole. Quickly taking up the bolee and the basket, he hurried to the well, calling his father. When he heard no answer, climbing the mound of dirt, he looked down inside the hole. Now the hole was much deeper, but there still wasn't any water in it. His father sat at the bottom of the hole; with his hands holding the fork, his head bent slightly to the right, Gobinah stared unblinkingly at the sky.

"Ay, bap!" the boy screamed.

But only a deep silence came out of the well.

THE SCHOONER *FLIGHT*

by **Derek Walcott**

Blanchisseuse

(Originally published in 1979)

1. Adios, Carenage

In idle August, while the sea soft,
and leaves of brown islands stick to the rim
of this Caribbean, I blow out the light
by the dreamless face of Maria Concepcion
to ship as a seaman on the schooner *Flight*.
Out in the yard turning gray in the dawn,
I stood like a stone and nothing else move
but the cold sea rippling like galvanize
and the nail holes of stars in the sky roof,
till a wind start to interfere with the trees.
I pass me dry neighbor sweeping she yard
as I went downhill, and I nearly said:
"Sweep soft, you witch, 'cause she don't sleep hard,"
but the bitch look through me like I was dead.
A route taxi pull up, park-lights still on.
The driver size up my bags with a grin:
"This time, Shabine, like you really gone!"
I ain't answer the ass, I simply pile in
the back seat and watch the sky burn
above Laventille pink as the gown
in which the woman I left was sleeping,

and I look in the rearview and see a man
exactly like me, and the man was weeping
for the houses, the streets, that whole fucking island.

Christ have mercy on all sleeping things!
From that dog rotting down Wrightson Road
to when I was a dog on these streets;
if loving these islands must be my load,
out of corruption my soul takes wings.
But they had started to poison my soul
with their big house, big car, big-time bohbohl,
coolie, nigger, Syrian, and French Creole,
so I leave it for them and their carnival—
I taking a sea bath, I gone down the road.
I know these islands from Monos to Nassau,
a rusty head sailor with sea-green eyes
that they nickname Shabine, the patois for
any red nigger, and I, Shabine, saw
when these slums of empire was paradise.
I'm just a red nigger who love the sea,
I had a sound colonial education,
I have Dutch, nigger, and English in me,
and either I'm nobody, or I'm a nation,

But Maria Concepcion was all my thought
watching the sea heaving up and down
as the port side of dories, schooners, and yachts
was painted afresh by the strokes of the sun
signing her name with every reflection;
I knew when dark-haired evening put on
her bright silk at sunset, and, folding the sea,
sidled under the sheet with her starry laugh,

that there'd be no rest, there'd be no forgetting.
Is like telling mourners round the graveside
about resurrection, they want the dead back,
so I smile to myself as the bow rope untied
and the *Flight* swing seaward: "Is no use repeating
that the sea have more fish. I ain't want her
dressed in the sexless light of a seraph,
I want those round brown eyes like a marmoset, and
till the day when I can lean back and laugh,
those claws that tickled my back on sweating
Sunday afternoons, like a crab on wet sand."
As I worked, watching the rotting waves come
past the bow that scissor the sea like silk,
I swear to you all, by my mother's milk,
by the stars that shall fly from tonight's furnace,
that I loved them, my children, my wife, my home;
I loved them as poets love the poetry
that kills them, as drowned sailors the sea.

You ever look up from some lonely beach
and see a far schooner? Well, when I write
this poem, each phrase go be soaked in salt;
I go draw and knot every line as tight
as ropes in this rigging; in simple speech
my common language go be the wind,
my pages the sails of the schooner *Flight*.
But let me tell you how this business begin.

2. Raptures of the Deep

Smuggled Scotch for O'Hara, big government man,
between Cedros and the Main, so the Coast Guard couldn't

      touch us,
and the Spanish pirogues always met us halfway,
but a voice kept saying: "Shabine, see this business
of playing pirate?" Well, so said, so done!
That whole racket crash. And I for a woman,
for her laces and silks, Maria Concepcion.
Ay, ay! Next thing I hear, some Commission of Inquiry
was being organized to conduct a big quiz,
with himself as chairman investigating himself.
Well, I knew damn well who the suckers would be,
not that shark in shark skin, but his pilot fish,
khaki-pants red niggers like you and me.
What worse, I fighting with Maria Concepcion,
plates flying and thing, so I swear: "Not again!"
It was mashing up my house and my family.
I was so broke all I needed was shades and a cup
or four shades and four cups in four-cup Port of Spain;
all the silver I had was the coins on the sea.

You saw them ministers in *The Express*,
guardians of the poor—one hand at their back,
and one set o' police only guarding their house,
and the Scotch pouring in through the back door.
As for that minister-monster who smuggled the booze,
that half-Syrian saurian, I got so vex to see
that face thick with powder, the warts, the stone lids
like a dinosaur caked with primordial ooze
by the lightning of flashbulbs sinking in wealth,
that I said: "Shabine, this is shit, understand!"
But he get somebody to kick my crutch out his office
like I was some artist! That bitch was so grand,
couldn't get off his high horse and kick me himself.

I have seen things that would make a slave sick
in this Trinidad, the Limers' Republic.

I couldn't shake the sea noise out of my head,
the shell of my ears sang Maria Concepcion,
so I start salvage diving with a crazy Mick,
name O'Shaugnessy, and a limey named Head;
but this Caribbean so choke with the dead
that when I would melt in emerald water,
whose ceiling rippled like a silk tent,
I saw them corals: brain, fire, sea fans,
dead-men's-fingers, and then, the dead men.
I saw that the powdery sand was their bones
ground white from Senegal to San Salvador,
so, I panic third dive, and surface for a month
in the Seamen's Hostel. Fish broth and sermons.
When I thought of the woe I had brought my wife,
when I saw my worries with that other woman,
I wept under water, salt seeking salt,
for her beauty had fallen on me like a sword
cleaving me from my children, flesh of my flesh!

There was this barge from St. Vincent, but she was too deep
to float her again. When we drank, the limey
got tired of my sobbing for Maria Concepcion.
He said he was getting the bends. Good for him!
The pain in my heart for Maria Concepcion,
the hurt I had done to my wife and children,
was worse than the bends. In the rapturous deep
there was no cleft rock where my soul could hide
like the boobies each sunset, no sandbar of light
where I could rest, like the pelicans know,

so I got raptures once, and I saw God
like a harpooned grouper bleeding, and a far
voice was rumbling, "Shabine, if you leave her,
if you leave her, I shall give you the morning star."
When I left the madhouse I tried other women
but, once they stripped naked, their spiky cunts
bristled like sea eggs and I couldn't dive.
The chaplain came round. I paid him no mind.
Where is my rest place, Jesus? Where is my harbor?
Where is the pillow I will not have to pay for,
and the window I can look from that frames my life?

3. *Shabine Leaves the Republic*

I had no nation now but the imagination.
After the white man, the niggers didn't want me
when the power swing to their side.
The first chain my hands and apologize, "History";
the next said I wasn't black enough for their pride.
Tell me, what power, on these unknown rocks—
a spray-plane Air Force, the Fire Brigade,
the Red Cross, the Regiment, two, three police dogs
that pass before you finish bawling "Parade!"?
I met History once, but he ain't recognize me,
a parchment Creole, with warts
like an old sea bottle, crawling like a crab
through the holes of shadow cast by the net
of a grille balcony; cream linen, cream hat.
I confront him and shout, "Sir, is Shabine!
They say I'se your grandson. You remember Grandma,
your black cook, at all?" The bitch hawk and spat.
A spit like that worth any number of words.

But that's all them bastards have left us: words.

I no longer believed in the revolution.
I was losing faith in the love of my woman.
I had seen that moment Aleksandr Blok
crystallize in *The Twelve*. Was between
the Police Marine Branch and Hotel Venezuelana
one Sunday at noon. Young men without flags
using shirts, their chests waiting for holes.
They kept marching into the mountains, and
their noise ceased as foam sinks into sand.
They sank in the bright hills like rain, every one
with his own nimbus, leaving shirts in the street,
and the echo of power at the end of the street.
Propeller-blade fans turn over the Senate;
the judges, they say, still sweat in carmine,
on Frederick Street the idlers all marching
by standing still, the Budget turns a new leaf.
In the 12:30 movies the projectors best
not break down, or you go see revolution. Aleksandr Blok
enters and sits in the third row of pit eating chocolate cone, waiting for a spaghetti Western with Clint Eastwood and featuring Lee Van Cleef.

4. *The* Flight, *Passing Blanchisseuse*

Dusk. The *Flight* passing Blanchisseuse.
Gulls wheel like from a gun again,
and foam gone amber that was white,
lighthouse and star start making friends,
down every beach the long day ends,
and there, on that last stretch of sand,

on a beach bare of all but light,
dark hands start pulling in the seine
of the dark sea, deep, deep inland.

5. *Shabine Encounters the Middle Passage*

Man, I brisk in the galley first thing next dawn,
brewing li'l coffee; fog coil from the sea
like the kettle steaming when I put it down
slow, slow, 'cause I couldn't believe what I see:
where the horizon was one silver haze,
the fog swirl and swell into sails, so close
that I saw it was sails, my hair grip my skull,
it was horrors, but it was beautiful.
We float through a rustling forest of ships
with sails dry like paper, behind the glass
I saw men with rusty eyeholes like cannons,
and whenever their half-naked crews cross the sun,
right through their tissue, you traced their bones
like leaves against the sunlight; frigates, barkentines,
the backward-moving current swept them on,
and high on their decks I saw great admirals,
Rodney, Nelson, de Grasse, I heard the hoarse orders
they gave those Shabines, and that forest
of masts sail right through the *Flight*,
and all you could hear was the ghostly sound
of waves rustling like grass in a low wind
and the hissing weeds they trailed from the stern;
slowly they heaved past from east to west
like this round world was some cranked water wheel,
every ship pouring like a wooden bucket
dredged from the deep; my memory revolve

on all sailors before me, then the sun
heat the horizon's ring and they was mist.

Next we pass slave ships. Flags of all nations,
our fathers below deck too deep, I suppose,
to hear us shouting. So we stop shouting. Who knows
who his grandfather is, much less his name?
Tomorrow our landfall will be the Barbados.

6. *The Sailor Sings Back to the Casuarinas*

You see them on the low hills of Barbados
bracing like windbreaks, needles for hurricanes,
trailing, like masts, the cirrus of torn sails;
when I was green like them, I used to think
those cypresses, leaning against the sea,
that take the sea noise up into their branches,
are not real cypresses but casuarinas.
Now captain just call them Canadian cedars.
But cedars, cypresses, or casuarinas,
whoever called them so had a good cause,
watching their bending bodies wail like women
after a storm, when some schooner came home
with news of one more sailor drowned again.
Once the sound "cypress" used to make more sense
than the green "casuarinas," though, to the wind
whatever grief bent them was all the same,
since they were trees with nothing else in mind
but heavenly leaping or to guard a grave;
but we live like our names and you would have
to be colonial to know the difference,
to know the pain of history words contain,

to love those trees with an inferior love,
and to believe: "Those casuarinas bend
like cypresses, their hair hangs down in rain
like sailors' wives. They're classic trees, and we,
if we live like the names our masters please,
by careful mimicry might become men."

7. *The* Flight *Anchors in Castries Harbor*

When the stars self were young over Castries,
I loved you alone and I loved the whole world.
What does it matter that our lives are different?
Burdened with the loves of our different children?
When I think of your young face washed by the wind
and your voice that chuckles in the slap of the sea?
The lights are out on La Toc promontory,
except for the hospital. Across at Vigie
the marina arcs keep vigil. I have kept my own
promise, to leave you the one thing I own,
you whom I loved first: my poetry.
We here for one night. Tomorrow, the *Flight* will be gone.

8. *Fight with the Crew*

It had one bitch on board, like he had me mark—
that was the cook, some Vincentian arse
with a skin like a gommier tree, red peeling bark,
and wash-out blue eyes; he wouldn't give me a ease,
like he feel he was white. Had an exercise book,
this same one here, that I was using to write
my poetry, so one day this man snatch it
from my hand, and start throwing it left and right

to the rest of the crew, bawling out, "Catch it,"
and start mincing me like I was some hen
because of the poems. Some case is for fist,
some case is for tholing pin, some is for knife—
this one was for knife. Well, I beg him first,
but he keep reading, "O my children, my wife,"
and playing he crying, to make the crew laugh;
it move like a flying fish, the silver knife
that catch him right in the plump of his calf,
and he faint so slowly, and he turn more white
than he thought he was. I suppose among men
you need that sort of thing. It ain't right
but that's how it is. There wasn't much pain,
just plenty blood, and Vincie and me best friend,
but none of them go fuck with my poetry again.

9. *Maria Concepcion & the Book of Dreams*

The jet that was screeching over the *Flight*
was opening a curtain into the past.
"Dominica ahead!"

                    "It still have Caribs there."
"One day go be planes only, no more boat."
"Vince, God ain't make nigger to fly through the air."
"Progress, Shabine, that's what it's all about.
Progress leaving all we small islands behind."
I was at the wheel, Vince sitting next to me
gaffing. Crisp, bracing day. A high-running sea.
"Progress is something to ask Caribs about.
They kill them by millions, some in war,
some by forced labor dying in the mines
looking for silver, after that niggers; more

progress. Until I see definite signs
that mankind change, Vince, I ain't want to hear.
Progress is history's dirty joke.
Ask that sad green island getting nearer."
Green islands, like mangoes pickled in brine.
In such fierce salt let my wound be healed,
me, in my freshness as a seafarer.
That night, with the sky sparks frosty with fire,
I ran like a Carib through Dominica,
my nose holes choked with memory of smoke;
I heard the screams of my burning children,
I ate the brains of mushrooms, the fungi
of devil's parasols under white, leprous rocks;
my breakfast was leaf mold in leaking forests,
with leaves big as maps, and when I heard noise
of the soldiers' progress through the thick leaves,
though my heart was bursting, I get up and ran
through the blades of balisier sharper than spears;
with the blood of my race, I ran, boy, I ran
with moss-footed speed like a painted bird;
then I fall, but I fall by an icy stream under
cool fountains of fern, and a screaming parrot
catch the dry branches and I drowned at last
in big breakers of smoke; then when that ocean
of black smoke pass, and the sky turn white,
there was nothing but Progress, if Progress is
an iguana as still as a young leaf in sunlight.
I bawl for Maria, and her *Book of Dreams*.

It anchored her sleep, that insomniac's Bible,
a soiled orange booklet with a cyclop's eye
center, from the Dominican Republic.

Its coarse pages were black with the usual
symbols of prophecy, in excited Spanish;
an open palm upright, sectioned and numbered
like a butcher chart, delivered the future.
One night, in a fever, radiantly ill,
she say, "Bring me the book, the end has come."
She said: "I dreamt of whales and a storm,"
but for that dream, the book had no answer.
A next night I dreamed of three old women
featureless as silkworms, stitching my fate,
and I scream at them to come out my house,
and I try beating them away with a broom,
but as they go out, so they crawl back again,
until I start screaming and crying, my flesh
raining with sweat, and she ravage the book
for the dream meaning, and there was nothing;
my nerves melt like a jellyfish—that was when I broke—
they found me round the Savannah, screaming:

All you see me talking to the wind, so you think I mad.
Well, Shabine has bridled the horses of the sea;
you see me watching the sun till my eyeballs seared,
so all you mad people feel Shabine crazy,
but all you ain't know my strength, hear? The coconuts
standing by in their regiments in yellow khaki,
they waiting for Shabine to take over these islands,
and all you best dread the day I am healed
of being a human. All you fate in my hand,
ministers, businessmen, Shabine have you, friend,
I shall scatter your lives like a handful of sand,
I who have no weapon but poetry and
the lances of palms and the sea's shining shield!

10. *Out of the Depths*

Next day, dark sea. A arse-aching dawn.
"Damn wind shift sudden as a woman mind."
The slow swell start cresting like some mountain range
with snow on the top.
                    "Ay, Skipper, sky dark!"
"This ain't right for August."
                    "This light damn strange,
this season, sky should be clear as a field."

A stingray steeplechase across the sea,
tail whipping water, the high man-o'-wars
start reeling inland, quick, quick an archery
of flying fish miss us! Vince say: "You notice?"
and a black-mane squall pounce on the sail
like a dog on a pigeon, and it snap the neck
of the *Flight* and shake it from head to tail.
"Be Jesus, I never see sea get so rough
so fast! That wind come from God back pocket!"
"Where Cap'n headin? Like the man gone blind!"
"If we's to drong, we go drong, Vince, fock-it!"
"Shabine, say your prayers, if life leave you any!"

I have not loved those that I loved enough.
Worse than the mule kick of Kick-'Em-Jenny
Channel, rain start to pelt the *Flight* between
mountains of water. If I was frighten?
The tent poles of water spouts bracing the sky
start wobbling, clouds unstitch at the seams
and sky water drench us, and I hear myself cry,

"I'm the drowned sailor in her *Book of Dreams*."
I remembered them ghost ships, I saw me corkscrewing
to the sea bed of sea worms, fathom pass fathom,
my jaw clench like a fist, and only one thing
hold me, trembling, how my family safe home.
Then a strength like it seize me and the strength said:
"I from backward people who still fear God."
Let Him, in His might, heave Leviathan upward
by the winch of His will, the beast pouring lace
from his sea-bottom bed; and that was the faith
that had fade from a child in the Methodist chapel
in Chisel Street, Castries, when the whale-bell
sang service and, in hard pews ribbed like the whale,
proud with despair, we sang how our race
survive the sea's maw, our history, our peril,
and now I was ready for whatever death will.
But if that storm had strength, was in Cap'n face,
beard beading with spray, tears salting his eyes,
crucify to his post, that nigger hold fast
to that wheel, man, like the cross held Jesus,
and the wounds of his eyes like they crying for us,
and I feeding him white rum, while every crest
with Leviathan-lash make the *Flight* quail
like two criminal. Whole night, with no rest,
till red-eyed like dawn, we watch our travail
subsiding, subside, and there was no more storm.
And the noon sea get calm as Thy Kingdom come.

11. After the Storm

There's a fresh light that follows a storm
while the whole sea still havoc; in its bright wake

I saw the veiled face of Maria Concepcion
marrying the ocean, then drifting away
in the widening lace of her bridal train
with white gulls her bridesmaids, till she was gone.
I wanted nothing after that day.
Across my own face, like the face of the sun,
a light rain was falling, with the sea calm.

Fall gently, rain, on the sea's upturned face
like a girl showering; make these islands fresh
as Shabine once knew them! Let every trace,
every hot road, smell like clothes she just press
and sprinkle with drizzle. I finish dream;
whatever the rain wash and the sun iron:
the white clouds, the sea and sky with one seam,
is clothes enough for my nakedness.
Though my *Flight* never pass the incoming tide
of this inland sea beyond the loud reefs
of the final Bahamas, I am satisfied
if my hand gave voice to one people's grief.
Open the map. More islands there, man,
than peas on a tin plate, all different size,
one thousand in the Bahamas alone,
from mountains to low scrub with coral keys,
and from this bowsprit, I bless every town,
the blue smell of smoke in hills behind them,
and the one small road winding down them like twine
to the roofs below; I have only one theme:

The bowsprit, the arrow, the longing, the lunging heart—
the flight to a target whose aim we'll never know,
vain search for one island that heals with its harbor

and a guiltless horizon, where the almond's shadow
doesn't injure the sand. There are so many islands!
As many islands as the stars at night
on that branched tree from which meteors are shaken
like falling fruit around the schooner *Flight*.
But things must fall, and so it always was,
on one hand Venus, on the other Mars;
fall, and are one, just as this earth is one
island in archipelagoes of stars.
My first friend was the sea. Now, is my last.
I stop talking now. I work, then I read,
cotching under a lantern hooked to the mast.
I try to forget what happiness was,
and when that don't work, I study the stars.
Sometimes is just me, and the soft-scissored foam
as the deck turn white and the moon open
a cloud like a door, and the light over me
is a road in white moonlight taking me home.
Shabine sang to you from the depths of the sea.

MALGRÉTOUTE

BY LAWRENCE SCOTT

Malgrétoute

(Originally published in 1987)

"Boy, when cocoa was king." That's what they used to say. Then the estate had begun to die. In his textbook on tropical agriculture, *Diseases of Crop-Plants in the Lesser Antilles* by W. Nowell, Mr. Wainwright remembered the description. It was a fungus which had come on the winds from Suriname on the South American mainland.

"Look, boss," Bosoon, the groom, pointed out the young cocoa tree near the verandah of the house at La Mariana. "Look, in the fork of the branch." It was a bruise on the bark of the tree. By the next day several shoots had appeared and by the end of the week they were a mass of interlacing twigs. Witchbroom. Then the leaves of the young tree had died after becoming soft and flimsy and the other shoots were grossly deformed. "Boy, when cocoa was king."

"When cocoa was king?" He could hardly remember. The damp morning air made him brace himself and rub his forearms vigorously; rub some warmth into the bones which were already arthritic in the elbows. Forty was not too old, he thought, made him think of death, though. He could start over again. Malgrétoute. This was where they had dumped him. Look at it, he thought. Each morning it was there as he stood at the top of the steps on the gallery, looking out over the sugar-cane estate on the edge of the gulf down by

Mosquito Creek into which the stinking Cipero River seeped, clogged with the refuse from the black galvanised barrack-rooms huddled in the gully encircling the junior overseer's house. A junior overseer, this was what he had become. He surveyed the scene like this each morning, each and every morning since he had arrived at Malgrétoute, in this fraction of the dawn, this half an hour which was his before his wife and children got up and before the servants began to pester his wife. This was it, a junior overseer on a run-down sugar-cane estate. "Boy, when cocoa was king."

He pushed open the Demerara window by the kitchen sink, filled the kettle with water and lit the wick of the kerosene stove. He couldn't die now. No. He couldn't die now. He didn't believe that. There was more, much more ahead, he thought, in spite of all that had happened, there must be more ahead. And then he thought of the sleeping children, six of them, and his wife. No. He didn't want them getting up now. This was his time, his half an hour. The flame went out and he had to light the wick again. The black sooty smoke curled off the dirty wick and caught the back of his throat. While the kettle began to boil he went down the rickety back stairs across the back yard to the latrine under the kimeet tree. As he approached the hut he inhaled the heady, strong perfume which came from the white wild lilies which liked to grow in the moist seepage behind the latrine. As he peed he wondered at this apparent contradiction in nature, how the wild lilies with their satiny petals opening out of shiny green stems, already beginning to unfurl to the first light and warmth, amidst the thick fleshy leaves, and reveal their golden centres with their dusty stamens of pollen, had chosen the nastiest place to grow and startle the world. As he buttoned up his crotch he wondered at that. No, he wouldn't die. "Bosoon, Bosoon, is that you?"

"Yes, boss."

"It's cold, boy."

"Yes, boss, it cold no arse. Excuse, excuse, boss. It cold like hell."

"No, Bosoon. You're right, it cold no tail. It damp." He could talk to Bosoon. The groom came out from under the house muffled up against the damp. Bosoon had come with him from La Mariana. He knew that Bosoon would stand by him. The black man would stand by him. He knew that.

Bosoon had grown up at La Mariana and picked cocoa for his father as a boy. Bosoon was his groom and now at Malgrétoute he was the watchman too, and then he didn't have anywhere to live, so he lived under the house. Bosoon would always be there. He didn't like his wife calling Bosoon to take messages in the shop. Bosoon was his man.

"Things still bad, eh, boss?"

"Yes, Bosoon, things still bad."

"I don't understand this thing, boss, no promotion except into dead man's boots. That is what he does say. The big manager man, how he not call you yet? Them is English people, boss, they don't understand. This thing gone back a long way. Gone back a long way, yes. You and me, me and you, me and your father. That is a long time, yes, boss. You going to have to kill somebody."

"Here, Bosoon, drink it while it's hot and strong." Mr. Wainwright laughed. Bosoon lit a cigarette and stood outside at the top of the back steps. Mr. Wainwright stood in the doorway and the two men were wrapped in the smoke and the steam and the aroma of the tea. "Yes, Bosoon, it's a long time."

"I go stay, boss. I not moving unless you move."

When he put the cup of tea on the bedside table, moving the rosary beads with his fingers as he placed the cup and saucer down, Mr. Wainwright decided again that he would go and see Robertson the G.M. He would go to the General Office and he would get Bosoon to ride with him. Bosoon liked to ride. He could ride Hope while Mr. Wainwright rode Prudence. "Tea, dear." He looked at his wife and saw six children and he couldn't really remember how it had come to this or for that matter how it had been. He didn't like to think now about how it had been. He still had a picture of her in his Bible when she was sixteen, long before he knew her. He looked at her now and saw his six children. It made him feel guilty that he didn't feel like that now as he had then. They didn't really talk, but they had an understanding. She was feeling it too as she still sat under the mosquito net, dangling her feet onto the damp pitchpine floor, feeling it every single day. She was feeling it too, the change, the disappointment; a disappointment for him though not in him. At least he didn't think it was in him, though at times he wondered, like last night when her brothers came out for a drink and everyone had drunk a lot of rum.

"You are the junior overseer on a run-down sugar-cane estate. What are we now?" She had got confidence from her brothers to say that and they too were sticking in their oars.

"Come on, man, get into business, man, agriculture is a dead end and cocoa dead, boy."

"When cocoa was king," the other brother laughed as he took another swig of rum. "When cocoa was king."

"Now is the motor-car, boy. No cocoa, no sugar. What you want to stay in this dump for and work for a set of limey people?"

He looked at his wife and saw six children.

"You can sell any blasted thing to the Americans on the base, and there is oil, man, the new El Dorado. You didn't know that is what they come here for originally, gold. Well, that is the new gold, El Dorado, oil."

He wasn't going to sell any blasted motor-cars and he wasn't going to be a salesman. He was a planter. His overseers knew him as a planter. They knew what he stood for. He stood for fairness, or for a kind of justice, an old justice when everything had its place. He worked hard and his men worked hard. They knew where they stood and he knew what he was, a manager, a planter on his father's cocoa estate. No, he wasn't going to go the way of his wife's brothers, become a businessman and live in a house in town. He wasn't going to leave the land and he wasn't going to stop managing and growing on this land. Bosoon, that was all he had left now, Bosoon. Bosoon would stay by him. Yes, he would take Bosoon this afternoon and go to Robertson. He could hear Robertson as he had heard him before. "No promotion, except into the boots of a dead man." Well he wasn't going to die and he wasn't going to wait for anyone else to die. He felt a new confidence as he walked across the drawing-room and began opening up the house. There was just the slightest discernible limp as he crossed the room with the heavy mahogany furniture standing all around him. The children from the barracks used to call him cork foot. He had had polio as a child. He opened up the Demerara windows and let the light, now that the dawn was over, lift the pall off the couch, the sideboard, the oval table with the six chairs, the cabinet and the trolley. They too had come with Bosoon from another place, from La Mariana.

He nearly cut himself shaving. He stirred some more lather into the wooden shaving-bowl and brushed it into his growth. He was afraid of these new hopes. There had been mornings like this before when he had noticed the lilies and gained hope and had had a good smoke with Bosoon and talked of old times. This had lifted him up, especially when Bosoon had made his promise, as he had done many times before, that he would stay and that he would not leave him. There had been times like this before. He could hear his wife fussing over the children and shooing the flies off the food on the breakfast table. Flies. Dysentery. "Sybil, cover the food, girl." The mesh of the window screens was ripped and the flies came in hordes and alighted on the food and the baby's bottles and the little boy was down with dysentery. That was all there, just the other side of the door. He could hear his wife pestering the cook that the maid had been late again. He was getting to look old, he thought, as he saw his masked face in the mirror. No, he was the same. There was a way in which you didn't notice how you were changing and then all of a sudden you could see it. An older man. Well, there could be dignity in that. He had seen his father grow with dignity, tall, silver-haired and a planter gone before him. He wasn't going to sell any blasted motor-cars. A thought crossed his mind that his sons would leave the land. Maybe it would be oil for them, maybe he was the last. "No promotion except into dead men's boots."

When it was after lunch and Sybil was brushing the crumbs off the dining-room table and a silence which was the silence of midday heat and the only sounds were the creaks of the wooden house, Bosoon came up the gravel road from the estate yard with two horses and tethered them under the mango tree at the front of the house.

"I leave it in God's hands," Mr. Wainwright's wife said to herself or her husband as she lay next to him on the big brass bed, resting. "I leave it in God's hands." The perfume of the wild lilies rose with the heat from the yard below the bedroom window. "I must pick some lilies for Father Sebastian and ask him to get Mrs. Goveia to put them on Our Lady's altar."

This was one of the first thoughts which Mr. Wainwright had as he and Bosoon rode out of the yard on their way to the general manager's office, imagining his wife with the wild lilies in her arms going into the town to see Father Sebastian. She had her priests. Something was on her mind. He had seen in her eyes the signs of a pilgrimage as she left the house; someone with a purpose to her visit and the lilies were an offering. She was lucky the way she could assail the gates of heaven. She made him feel it was a kind of battle. He remembered standing once outside the bedroom door when she and the children were saying the family rosary and he remembered the prayer which he heard his wife reciting, "armies set in battle array." For him the lilies were wild and belonged in the dawn where he could see them when he went to pee. For his wife they were an offering to supplicate and adorn the Virgin Mary's altar for some intention. She had her own intentions this afternoon.

They had their different journeys, he thought. Once, too, she was wild and black-haired with deep brown eyes. Once, too, she had been wild.

The two men didn't talk and Bosoon rode just behind on Hope; Mr. Wainwright was on his favourite horse, Prudence.

"Wainwright." He had been asked to wait on the gallery outside the G.M.'s office overlooking the factory. Then he was called. Robertson was a fat man in a brown suit with a collar and tie which didn't suit the climate and he was red-faced and sweaty. His white skin puckered in the folds of flesh around the collar. "Good to see you, my good man. Come in and have a seat." He indicated the leather-upholstered chair in front of the general manager's desk. Above, the ceiling fan whirled and hummed, making the papers flutter on the desk. "Well,

what can I do for you? You've come all this way from Malgrétoute. What can I do?"

It always took Mr. Wainwright a while to believe that this
was true: that these words were in fact what the G.M. actually meant, because they were exactly the same each time,
pretending in their insinuation that he, Mr. Wainwright, had
never been here before and that Robertson himself was a complete innocent, there, for him, had given up his afternoon entirely to listen to him as if he had never listened to him before,
hadn't an inkling what it was Mr. Wainwright had ridden all
the way from Malgrétoute for. At first he did not know what
to say, how to speak the truth in the face of someone who was
lying. Wainwright knew that Robertson was a liar. He waited
for him to stop lying, which eventually he did, reluctantly.

"Well, Wainwright, you know it has nothing to do with
me. You know that, don't you?'

Mr. Wainwright didn't reply. He stared at Robertson. He
wasn't going to respond to lies. He wondered whether God,
in whose hands this all was, would actually look down, as his
wife seemed to indicate, surveying the two men, and would
somehow inspire Robertson to tell the truth. Maybe the Holy
Ghost, to whom his wife was constantly appealing for wisdom,
and who could conveniently take the form of a dove, would
perhaps fly in through the open window and alight on Robertson's desk. Mr. Wainwright smiled ironically. "I leave it in
God's hands."

"You see, I can see that you know that, old man. It's those
people at the head office in the Strand. When the director
comes down in the summer I will put it to him."

"The summer?" Mr. Wainwright did not intend to speak.
"You mean August holidays?" It was a small assertion but Robertson took the point reluctantly as he wiped his brow and

then blew his nose into the same handkerchief. Mr. Wainwright was intolerant of people who didn't take care of personal hygiene. He himself looked fresh in front of Robertson in his Aertex shirt and pressed khaki pants. "We only have two seasons here and this is the dry season, a very dry season." Mr. Wainwright surprised himself. He didn't normally speak metaphorically. Maybe it was a way of avoiding, for the moment anyway, the direct confrontation which would eventually have to take place and it surprised him how Robertson could appear to forget the previous confrontations, but then he had not taken them far enough.

"Well, you know what I always say . . ."

"No promotion except into a dead man's boots," Mr. Wainwright quickly filled in.

"Quite," said Robertson.

"Well, who are you going to kill?" asked Mr. Wainwright.

"What?"

"Who are you going to kill?" Mr. Wainwright could hear Bosoon that morning. He could still taste the tea and smell the wild lilies. He knew that Bosoon would be just outside sitting at the bottom of the concrete steps. Uncharacteristically Mr. Wainwright started to laugh out loud over and over again. "No promotion except into a dead man's boots. Well, you're going to have to kill somebody, that is what I'm telling you, and if you don't kill somebody, well, you never know what might happen." He began to laugh again, got up and walked around Robertson's office. He didn't take any notice of Robertson. He opened the office door and shouted, "Bosoon!"

"Now, Wainwright, nothing stupid."

Bosoon ran up the stairs and was at the door in a minute. "Yes, boss?"

"The horses. I've just told Mr. Robertson that he will have to kill somebody. He will have to find me a pair of boots."

"Yes, boss."

"Wainwright."

"Next time you call me, Robertson, I want to hear that you have a pair of boots for me and I don't want to know who the dead man is."

In the yard at Malgrétoute Bosoon said, "You get him, boss, you get him. He didn't know what hit him. Is what I told you this morning. He going to have to kill somebody."

That evening Mr. Wainwright noticed that his wife didn't speak and she didn't ask how he had got on. He felt that he couldn't really tell her what he had said. It now seemed too extravagant and quite crazy and out of character what he had said to Robertson. What had got into him?

The next morning, early, when he was still enjoying the smell of the lilies and Bosoon and himself were having their cup of tea on the back steps, the telephone rang and his wife answered it. It was Robertson. He said, "Wainwright, I've got you a pair of boots." Mr. Wainwright put down the receiver and looked at his wife. She started to cry and he said, "Don't worry, it's the Holy Ghost."

"No," she said, laughing behind her tears. "It's us, we're going to have another child."

ASSAM'S IRON CHEST

BY WILLI CHEN

Mayaro

(Originally published in 1988)

A dull moon glowed in the country-night darkness. They came out of hiding from behind the caimette tree, avoiding the crackle of dead leaves underfoot. Into the pale light stepped big, loudmouthed Mathias, Boyo with his matted dreadlocks wrapped up in a "Marvingay" hat, and laglee-chewing Sagamouth, so nicknamed because of his grotesque lips and the smattering noises they made.

In the little clearing overlooking Assam's shopyard, they waited patiently behind large tannia leaves that shielded them from the light of passing motorists. They waited for the last bus to rattle by on its return journey to town and for the soft glow of Assam's Coleman lamp, whirring moths and beetles striking against the lampshade, to go out.

Boyo puffed at the carmine-tipped stick of ganja that brightened his face as he slapped at mosquitoes. Sagamouth's lips continued slurping noisily.

"Keep quiet, man. Christ! You goh wake up the whole damn village," Mathias hissed between clenched teeth.

"Look, the light out," Sagamouth whispered excitedly.

"Yea, but keep your flapping mouth shut. I could see. Who in charge here? Boyo, put out that weed. Whole place stink ah grass," Mathias warned.

At the galvanized paling surrounding the shopyard, a

flimsy steel sheet suddenly loosened in the moonlight and fell aside, allowing three figures to squeeze through the narrow space into the shopyard. They were confronted by stacks of empty soft drink crates, discarded cartons, pitch oil tins and, against the shed, bundles of stacked crocus bags.

Remembering the action in the motion picture *Bataan*, and with the dramatic invasion in *Desert Fox* still fresh in his mind, Mathias crouched on all fours, leading his platoon across the yard.

"Sssh," he cautioned them as he sat on his buttocks before the big door. They paused in the darkness. Mathias's hands felt for the door frame. He inserted a pig foot into the crevice. With both feet against the wall he pried the door, throwing his whole weight on it. A slow cracking noise erupted as the nails lifted off the hinges and the door came up. A dank odour of wet oilmeal, soap and stale mackerel greeted them. They crawled in, feeling their way between the stacks of packaged goods. Further inside, they saw a table with a lighted lamp and a red spot of mosquito coil under it. A big square mosquito net hung over a four-poster bed out of which floated Assam's snores in grating spasms.

Convinced that Assam was sound asleep, Mathias struck a match and immediately shadows jumped across the walls, on the shelves of bottles and over tinned stuffs. On the floor, crowding the aisles, was the paraphernalia of jumbled haberdashery, pots and pans, and bags of peas and beans. Moving in the crowded interior, Mathias came to the room where, over a small table, bills hung pinned to the wall, next to a Chinese calendar. Cupping the lighted match in his hand, Mathias tiptoed farther inside. More bags, packed in rows, and bales of macaroni and cornmeal. Flagons of cider and an old rum cask stood on the floor. In the corner, the square block of metal stood on a rough framework of local timber; a squat, dull hunk of iron with a circular dial of brass. It was the iron chest. Mathias came up to it and tested its weight. Boyo braced himself in readiness.

With Sagamouth holding the light, Mathias and Boyo heaved at the heavy hulk of iron. They pushed until the wooden stand inched along the floor.

"Damn thing must be full," Boyo said.

"Cane farmer pay, choopid," Sagamouth replied, spraying them with his spittle.

"All you keep quiet," Mathias entreated.

Pitting themselves against the heavy load, they worked with caution. Twice they heard Assam cough. Their hands glided, slipped over the smooth surface of the chest. After some strenuous efforts, they managed to push the chest to the doorway. Finally the whole bulk of metal was heaved outside, catapulting, digging into the yard with a dull thud.

The cool night breeze invigorated their bodies. The sight of the chest inspired their minds with the promise of new things in life. Sagamouth disappeared into the bushes and returned with a crocus bag containing a crowbar, a sledgehammer and a flambeau. Behind him he dragged a large piece of board, the underside of which was lined with plain galvanized sheeting. At one end was tied a long piece of rope. They eased their cargo onto the wooden contraption. Mathias again directed the operations. Standing before the metal chest, he tied the end of the rope around his waist and leant forward. Boyo and Sagamouth were pushing at the rear.

They hauled the makeshift sledge along the grassy side tracks. With the heavy iron chest strapped to it, it skidded and scuttled across the bare ground. Their backs shone like their faces, which steamed with perspiration. Boyo puffed like a mule. Sagamouth's mouth continued its feeble movements. They halted behind a silk cotton tree. Mathias swung the axe in long, measured strokes against the chest. The sounds echoed deep into the woods. The heavy blows ricocheted over the door. Now and then he stopped to inspect the shallow indentations. The brass handle had fallen off, the dial long warped under the punishing blows. Yet the door remained sealed. They persevered, taking turns with the sledgehammer and crowbar, until Mathias, bringing the heavy hammer from high overhead, struck the chest with such force that they heard a loud cracking noise.

Instantly they sprang forward, their eager hands reached out for the door. Three pairs of hands churned inside the chest, as their eyes opened wide in anticipation. Then Saga-mouth withdrew, exclaiming, "Empty."

"Christ, you mean the damn thing en't have a cent, boy?"

"All dis damn trouble," Boyo said.

Mathias stood up wearily and looked at the others, his arms sore and wet, as he whispered, "Dat damn Chinese smart like hell! Ah never cud believe it. You mean he move out all de damn money, boy?"

Sagamouth's dribbling stopped. Boyo looked up at the sky.

One day, some three months afterwards, when the notorious episode was almost forgotten in the little village and the blue police van had long completed its trips to Assam's on investigation, Sagamouth came into Assam's shop. He stood at the counter and called for a pound of saltbeef. There was no one in the shop except for a well-dressed man. A briefcase was on the counter and he was busily scribbling on a pad.

"Yes, please sign on this, Mr. Assam," the man said in his mellow voice. Assam, spectacles tied to his ear with a piece of flour-bag string, leant over the counter and scrawled on the pad.

"Have everything dong, Mr. Blong?"

"Yes, all that you have told me," Mr. Brown replied. "$1,000 in US, $15,000 in Canadian and $2,100 in TT cash. $89 in silver and that solid gold chain from China. But as I said, I'm not sure that the company will pay the foreign money."

Assam placed a large brown paper bag containing two bottles of rum on the counter before Mr. Brown.

"Well, check all in TT dollars then," Assam said, taking out another brown bag from below the counter.

Mr. Brown smiled and pointed to the last item on the list. "Ah—that is the iron chest, Mr. Assam. The company will pay you the $8,000 you have claimed."

"Yes sah," Assam said smiling, "velly goot," his eyes two narrow slits behind thick lenses.

Sagamouth stood dumb, rooted in front of the counter, unmoving, as he listened to the conversation. His lips had suddenly lost all sense of movement. They hung droopily over the counter, nearly falling into the shop-scale pan.

JOEBELL AND AMERICA

BY EARL LOVELACE

Cunaripo

(Originally published in 1988)

One

Joebell find that he seeing too much hell in Trinidad so he make up his mind to leave and go away. The place he find he should go is America, where everybody have a motor-car and you could ski on snow and where it have seventy-five channels of colour television that never sign off and you could sit down and watch for days, all the boxing and wrestling and basketball, right there as it happening. Money is the one prob-lem that keeping him in Cunaripo; but that year as Christmas was coming, luck hit Joebell in the gamble, and for three days straight he win out the wappie. After he give two good pard-ners a stake and hand his mother a raise and buy a watch for his girl, he still have nineteen hundred and seventy-five Trini-dad and Tobago dollars that is his own. That was the time. If Joebell don't go to America now, he will never go again.

But a couple years earlier, Joebell make prison for a wound-ing, and before that they had him up for resisting arrest and using obscene language. Joebell have a record; and for him to get a passport he must first get a letter from the police to say that he is of good character. All the bribe Joebell try to bribe, he can't get this letter from the police. He prepare to pay a thousand dollars for the letter; but the police pardner who he had working on the matter keep telling him to come back and come back and come back. But another pardner tell him that with the same thousand dollars he could get a whole new American passport, with new name and everything. The only thing a little ticklish is Joebell will have to talk Yankee.

Joebell smile, because if is one gift he have it is to talk languages, not Spanish and French and Italian and such, but he could talk English and American and Grenadian and Jamaican; and of all of them the one he love best is American. If that is the only problem, well, Joebell in America already.

But it have another problem. The fellar who fixing up the passport business for him tell him straight, if he try to go direct from Trinidad to America with the US passport, he could get arrest at the Trinidad airport, so the pardner advise that the best thing to do is for Joebell to try to get in through Puerto Rico where they have all those Spanish people and where the immigration don't be so fussy. Matter fix. Joebell write another pardner who he went to school with and who in the States seven years, and tell him he coming over, to look out for him, he will ring him from Puerto Rico.

Up in Independence Recreation Club where we gamble, since Joebell win this big money, he is a hero. All the fellars is suddenly his friend, everybody calling out, "Joebell! Joebell!" some asking his opinion and some giving him advice on how to gamble his money. But Joebell not in no hurry. He know just as how you could win fast playing wappie, so you could lose fast too; and although he want to stay in the wappie room and hear how we talk up his gambling ability, he decide that the safer thing to do is to go and play poker where if he have to lose he could lose more slow and where if he lucky he could win a good raise too. Joebell don't really have to be in the gambling club at all. His money is his own; but Joebell have himself down as a hero, and to win and run away is not classy. Joebell have himself down as classy.

Fellars' eyes open big big that night when they see Joebell heading for the poker room, because in there it have Japan and Fisherman from Mayaro and Captain and Papoye and a fellar named Morgan who every Thursday does come up from Tunapuna with a paper bag full with money and a knife in his shoe. Every man in there could really play poker.

In wappie, luck is the master; but in poker, skill is what make luck work for you. When day break that Friday morning, Joebell stagger out the poker room with his whole body wash down with perspiration, out five hundred of his good dollars. Friday night he come back with the money he had give his girl to keep. By eleven he was down three. Fellars get silent and all of us vex to see how money he wait so long to get he giving away so easy. But Joebell was really to go America in truth. In the middle of the poker, he leave the game to pee. On his way back, he walk into the wappie room. If you see Joebell: the whole front of his shirt open and he wiping sweat from all behind his head. "Heat!" somebody laugh and say. On the table that time is two card: jack and trey. Albon and Ram was winning everybody. The both of them like trey. They gobbling up all bets. Was a Friday night. Waterworks get pay, County Council get pay. It had men from Forestry. It had fellars from the housing project. Money high high on the table. Joebell favourite card is Jack.

Ram was a loser the night Joebell win big; now, Ram on top.

"Who against trey!" Ram say. He don't look at Joebell, but everybody know is Joebell he talking to. Out of all Joebell money, one thousand gone to pay for the false passport, and already in the poker he lose eight. Joebell have himself down as a hero. A hero can't turn away. Everybody waiting to see. They talking, but they waiting to see what Joebell will do. Joebell wipe his face, then wipe his chest, then he wring out the perspiration from the handkerchief, fold the kerchief and put it round his neck, and bam, just like that, like how you see in pictures when the star boy, quiet all the time, begin to make his move, Joebell crawl right up the wappie table, fellars clearing the way for him, and he empty out everything he had in his two pocket, and, lazy lazy, like he really is that star boy, he say, "Jack for this money!"

Ram was waiting. "Count it, Casa," he say.

When they count the money, was two hundred and thirteen dollars and some change. Joebell throw the change for a broken hustler, Ram match him. Bam! Bam! Bam! In three card, jack play. "Double!" Joebell say. "For all," which mean that Joebell betting that another jack play before any trey.

Ram put some, and Albon put the rest, they sure is robbery.

Whap! Whap! Whap! Jack play. "Divine!" Joebell say. That night Joebell leave the club with fifteen hundred dollars. Fellars calling him the Gambler of Natchez.

When we see Joebell next, his beard shave off, his head cut in a GI trim, and he walking with a fast kinda shuffle, his body leaned forward and his hands in his pockets and he talking Yankee: "How ya doin, Main! Hi-ya, baby!" And then we don't see Joebell in Cunaripo.

"Joebell gone away," his mother, Miss Myrtle, say. "Praise God!"

If they have to give a medal for patience in Cunaripo, Miss Myrtle believe that the medal is hers just from the trials and tribulations she undergo with Joebell. Since he leave school his best friend is Trouble, and wherever Trouble is, right there is Joebell.

"I shoulda mind my child myself," she complain. "His grandmother spoil him too much, make him feel he is too much of a star, make him believe that the world too easy."

"The world don't owe you anything, boy," she tell him. "Try to be decent, son," she say. Is like a stick break in Joebell two ears, he don't hear a word she have to say. She talk to him. She ask his uncle Floyd to talk to him. She go by the priest in Mount St. Benedict to say a novena for him. She say the ninety-first psalm for him. She go by a obeah woman in Moruga to see what really happening to him. The obeah woman tell her to bring him quick so she could give him a bath and a guard to keep off the evil spirit that somebody have lighting on him. Joebell fly up in one big vexation with his mother for enticing him to go to the obeah woman: "Ma, what stupidness you trying to get me in? You know I don't believe in this negromancy business. What blight you want to fall on me now? That is why it so hard for me to win in gamble, you crossing up my luck."

But Miss Myrtle pray and she pray and at last, praise God, the answer come, not as how she did want it—you can't get everything the way you want it—but, praise God, Joebell gone away. And to those that close to her, she whisper, "America!" for that is the destination Joebell give her.

But Joebell ain't reach America yet. His girl Alicia, who working at Last Chance snackette on the Cunaripo road, is the only one he tell that Puerto Rico is the place he trying to get to. Since she take up with Joebell, her mother quarrelling with her every day, "How a nice girl like you could get in with such a vagabond fellar? You don't have eyes in your head to see that the boy is only trouble?" They talk to her, they tell her how he stab a man in the gambling club and went to jail. They tell her how he have this ugly beard and this ugly look in his face. They tell her how he don't work nowhere regular. "Child, why you bringing this cross into your life?" they ask her. They get her uncle Matthew to talk to her. They carry her to Mount St. Benedict for the priest to say a novena for her. They give her the ninety-first psalm to say. They carry her to Moruga to a obeah woman who bathe her in a tub with bush, and smoke incense all over her to untangle her mind from Joebell.

But there is a style about Joebell that she like. Is a dream in him that she see. And a sad craziness that make her sad too but in a happy kinda way. The first time she see him in the snackette, she watch him and don't say nothing, but she think, *Hey! Who he think he is?* He come in the snackette with this foolish grin on his face and this strolling walk and this kinda commanding way about him and sit down at the table with his legs wide open, taking up a big space as if he spending a hundred dollars, and all he ask for is a coconut roll and a juice. And then he call her again, this time he want a napkin and a toothpick. Napkins and toothpicks is for people who eating food; but she give them to him. And still he sit down there with some blight, some trouble hanging over him, looking for somebody to quarrel with or for something to get him vex so he could parade. She just do her work, and not a word she tell him. And just like that, just so by himself, he cool down and start talking to her though they didn't introduce.

Everything he talk about is big: big mountains and big cars and racehorses and heavyweight boxing champions and people in America—everything big. And she look at him from behind the counter and she see his sad craziness and she hear him talk about all this bigness far away, that make her feel too that she would like to go somewhere and be somebody, and just like that, without any words or touching, it begin.

Sometimes he'd come in the snackette, walking big and singing, and those times he'd be so broke all he could afford to call for'd be a glass of cold water. He wanted to be a calypsonian, he say; but he didn't have no great tune and his compositions wasn't so great either and everything he sing had a kinda sadness about it, no matter how he sing it. Before they start talking direct to one another he'd sing, closing his eyes and hunching his shoulders, and people in the snackette'd think he was just making joke; but she know the song was for her and she'd feel pretty and sad and think about places far away. He used to sing in a country-and-western style, this song, his own composition:

> *Gonna take ma baby*
> *Away on a trip*
> *Gonna take ma baby*
> *Yip yip yip*
> *We gonna travel far*
> *To New Orleans*
> *Me and ma baby*
> *Be digging the scene*

If somebody came in and had to be served, he'd stop singing while she served them, then he'd start up again. And just so, without saying anything or touching or anything, she was his girl.

She never tell him about the trouble she was getting at home because of him. In fact she hardly talk at all. She'd just sit there behind the counter and listen to him. He had another calypso that he thought would be a hit:

> *Look at Mahatma Ghandi*

Look at Hitler and Mussolini
Look at Uriah Butler
Look at Kwame Nkrumah
Great as they was
Every one of them had to stand the pressure

He used to take up the paper that was on one side of the counter and sit down and read it. "Derby day, " he would say. "Look at the horses running," and he would read out the horses' names. Or it would be boxing, and he would say Muhammad boxing today, or Sugar. He talked about these people as if they were personal friends of his.

One day he brought her five pounds of deer wrapped in a big brown paper bag. She was sure he pay a lot of money for it. "Put this in the fridge until you going home." Chenette, mangoes, oranges, sapodillas—he was always bringing things for her. When her mother ask her where she was getting these things, she tell her that the owner of the place give them to her. For her birthday Joebell bring her a big box wrapped in fancy paper and went away, so proud and shy, he couldn't stand to see her open it, and when she open it it was a vase with a whole bunch of flowers made from coloured feathers and a big birthday card with an inscription: *From guess who?*

"Now, who give you this? The owner?" her mother asked.

She had to make up another story.

When he was broke she would slip him a dollar or two of her own money, and if he win in the gamble he would give her some of the money to keep for him, but she didn't keep it long, he mostly always came back for it next day. And they didn't have to say anything to understand each other. He would just watch her and she would know from his face if he was broke and want a dollar or if he just drop in to see her, and he could tell from her face if she want him to stay away altogether that day or if he should make a turn and come again or what. He didn't get to go no place with her, 'cause in the night when the snackette close her big brother would be waiting to take her home.

"Thank God!" her mother say when she hear Joebell gone away. "Thank you, Master Jesus, for helping to deliver this child from the clutches of that vagabond." She was so happy she hold a thanksgiving feast, buy sweet drinks and make cake and invite all the neighbours' little children; and she was surprise that Alicia was smiling. But Alicia was thinking, *Lord, just please let him get to America, they will see who is vagabond. Lord, just let him get through that immigration, they will see happiness when he send for me.*

The fellars go round by the snackette where Alicia working and they ask for Joebell.

"Joebell gone away," she tell them.

"Gone away and leave a nice girl like you? If was me I would never leave you."

And she just smile that smile that make her look like she crying and she mumble something that don't mean nothing, but if you listen good is, *Well, is not you.*

"Why you don't let me take you to the dance in the centre Saturday? Joey Lewis playing. Why you don't come and forget that crazy fellar?"

But Alicia smile no, all the time thinking, *Wait until he send for me, you will see who crazy.* And she sell the cake and the coconut roll and sweet drink and mauby that they ask for and take their money and give them their change and move off with that soft, bright, drowsy sadness that stir fellars, that make them sit down and drink their sweet drink and eat their coconut roll and look at her face with the spread of her nose and the lips stretch across her mouth in a full round soft curve and her faraway eyes and think how lucky Joebell is.

When Joebell get the passport he look at the picture in it and he say, "Wait! This fellar ain't look like me. A blind man could see this is not me."

"I know you woulda say that," the pardner with the passport say. "You could see you don't know nothing about the American immigration. Listen, in America, every black face is the same to white people. They don't see no difference. And this fellar here is the same height as you, roughly the same age. That is what you have to think about, those little details, not how his face looking."

"You saying this is me, this fellar here is me?" Joebell ask again. "You want them to lock me up or what, man? This is what I pay a thousand dollars for? A lockup?"

"Look, you have no worry. I went America one time on a passport where the fellar had a beard and I was shave clean and they ain't question me. If you was white you mighta have a problem, but black, man, you easy."

And in truth when he think of it, Joebell could see the point, 'cause he ain't sure he could tell the difference between two Chinese.

"But wait!" Joebell say. "Suppose I meet up a black immigration?"

"Ah," the fellar say, "you thinking! Anyhow, it ain't have that many, but if you see one stay far from him."

So Joebell, with his passport in his pocket, get a fellar who running contraband to carry him to Venezuela where his brother was living. He decide to spend a couple days by his brother, and from there take a plane to Puerto Rico, in transit to America.

His brother had a job as a motor car mechanic.

"Why don't you stay here?" his brother say. "It have work here you could get. And TV does be on whole day."

"The TV in Spanish," Joebell tell him.

"You could learn Spanish."

"By the time I finish Spanish I is a old man," Joebell say. "*Caramba! Caramba! Habla! Habla!* No. And besides, I done pay my thousand dollars. I have my American passport. I is an American citizen. And," he whisper, softening just at the thought of her, "I have a girl who coming to meet me in America."

Joebell leave Venezuela in a brown suit that he get from his brother, a strong-looking pair of brown leather boots that he buy, with buckles instead of laces, a cowboy hat on his head and an old camera over his shoulder and in his mouth a cigar, and now he is James Armstrong Brady of the 125th Infantry regiment from Alabama, Vietnam veteran, twenty-six years old. And when he reach the airport in Puerto Rico he walk with a swagger and he puff his cigar like he already home in the United States of America. And not for one moment it don't strike Joebell that he doing any wrong.

No. Joebell believe the world is a hustle. He believe everybody running some game, putting on some show, and the only thing that separate people is that some have power and others don't have none, that who in in and who out out, and that is exactly what Joebell kick against, because Joebell have himself down as a hero too and he not prepare to sit down timid timid as if he stupid and see a set of bluffers take over the world, and he stay wasting away in Cunaripo; and that is Joebell's trouble. That is what people call his craziness, is that that mark him out. That is the "light" that the obeah woman in Moruga see burning on him, is that that frighten his mother and charm Alicia and make her mother want to pry her loose from him. Is that that fellars see when they see him throw down his last hundred dollars on a single card, as if he know it going to play. The thing is that Joebell really don't be betting on the card, Joebell does be betting on himself. He don't be trying to guess about which card is the right one, he is trying to find that power in himself that will make him call correct. And that power is what Joebell searching for as he queue up in the line leading to the immigration entering Puerto Rico. Is that power that he calling up in himself as he stand there, because if he can feel that power, if that power come inside him, then nothing could stop him. And now this was it.

"Mr. Brady?" the immigration man look up from Joebell passport and say, same time turning the leaves of the passport. And he glance at Joebell and look at the picture. And he take up another book and look in it, and look again at Joebell; and maybe it is that power Joebell reaching for, that thing inside him, his craziness that look like arrogance, that put a kinda sneer on his face that make the immigration man take another look.

"Vietnam veteran? Mr. Brady, where you coming from?"

"Venezuela."

The fellar ask a few more questions. He is asking Joebell more questions than he ask anybody.

"Whatsamatta? Watsa problem?" Joebell ask. "Man, I ain't never seen such incompetency as you got here. This is boring. Hey, I've got a plane to catch. I ain't got all day."

All in the airport people looking at Joebell 'cause Joebell not talking easy, and he biting his cigar so that his words coming to the immigration through his teeth. Why Joebell get on so is because Joebell believe that one of the main marks of a real American is that he don't stand no nonsense. Any time you get a real American in an aggravating situation, the first thing he do is let his voice be heard in objection: in other words, he does get on.

In fact, that is one of the things Joebell admire most about Americans: they like to get on. They don't care who hear them, they going to open their mouth and talk for their rights. So that is why Joebell get on so about incompetency and missing his plane and so on. Most fellars who didn't know what it was to be a real American woulda take it cool. Joebell know what he doing.

"Sir, please step into the first room on your right and take a seat until your name is called." Now is the immigration talking, and the fellar firm and he not frighten, 'cause he is American too. I don't know if Joebell realise that before he get on. That is the sort of miscalculation Joebell does make sometimes in gambling and in life.

"Maan, just you remember I gotta plane to catch," and Joebell step off with that slow, tall insolence like Jack Palance getting off his horse in *Shane*, but he take off his hat and go and sit down where the fellar tell him to sit down.

It had seven other people in the room but Joebell go and sit down by himself because with all the talk he talking big, Joebell just playing for time, just trying to put them off; and now he start figuring serious how he going to get through this one. And he feeling for that power, that craziness that sometimes take him over when he in a wappie game, when every bet he call he call right; and he telling himself they can't trap him with any question because he grow up in America right there in Trinidad. In his grandmother days was the British; but he know from Al Jolson to James Brown. He know Tallahatchie Bridge and Rocktown Mountain. He know Doris Day and Frank Sinatra. He know America. And Joebell settle himself down not bothering to remember anything, just call-ing up his power. And then he see this tall black fellar over six foot five enter the room. At a glance Joebell could tell he's a crook, and next thing he know is this fellar coming to sit down side of him.

Two

I sit down there by myself alone and I know they watching me. Everybody else in the room white. This black fellar come in the room, with beads of perspiration running down his face and his eyes wild and he looking round like he escape. As soon as I see him I say "Oh God!" because I know with all the empty seats all about the place is me he coming to. He don't know my troubles. He believe I want friends. I want to tell him, *Listen, man, I love you. I really dig my people, but now is not the time to come and talk to me. Go and be friendly by those other people, they could afford to be friends with you.* But I can't tell him that 'cause I don't want to offend him and I have to watch how I talking in case in my situation I slip from American to Trinidadian. He shake my hand in the Black Power sign. And we sit down there side by side, two crooks, he and me, unless he's a spy they send to spy on me.

I letting him do all the talking, I just nodding and saying, *Yeah, yeah.*

He's an American who just come out of jail in Puerto Rico for dope or something. He was in Vietnam too. He talking, but I really ain't listening to him. I thinking how my plane going. I thinking about Alicia and how sad her face will get when she don't get the letter that I suppose to send for her to come to America. I thinking about my mother and about the fellars up in Independence Recreation Club and around the wappie table when the betting slow, how they will talk about me, "Natchez," who win in the wappie and go to America—nobody ever do that before—and I thinking how nice it will be for me and Alicia after we spend some time in America to go back home to Trinidad for a holiday and stay in the Hilton and hire a big car and go to see her mother. I think about the Spanish I woulda have to learn if I did stay in Venezuela.

At last they call me inside another room. This time I go cool.

It have two fellars in this room, a big tough one with a stone face and a jaw like a steel trap, and a small brisk one with eyes like a squirrel. The small one is smoking a cigarette. The tough one is the one asking questions.

The small one just sit down there with his squirrel eyes watching me, and smoking his cigarette.

"What's your name?"

And I watching his jaw how they clamping down on the words. "Ma name is James Armstrong Brady."

"Age?"

And he go through a whole long set of questions.

"You're a Vietnam veteran, you say? Where did you train?"

And I smile 'cause I see enough war pictures to know. "Nor' Carolina," I say.

"Went to school there?"

I tell him where I went to school. He ask questions until I dizzy.

The both of them know I lying, and maybe they coulda just throw me in jail just so without no big interrogation; but, America. That is why I love America. They love a challenge. Something in my style is a challenge to them, and they just don't want to lock me up because they have the power, they want to trap me plain for even me to see. So now is me, Joebell, and these two Yankees. And I waiting, 'cause I grow up on

John Wayne and Gary Cooper and Audie Murphy and James Stewart and Jeff Chandler. I know the Dodgers and Phillies, the Redskins and the Dallas Cowboys, Green Bay Packers and the Vikings. I know Walt Frazier and Doctor J, and Bill Russell and Wilt Chamberlain. Really, in truth, I know America so much, I feel American. Is just that I ain't born there.

As fast as the squirrel-eye one finish smoke one cigarette, he light another. He ain't saying nothing, only listening. At last he put out his cigarette, he say, "Recite the alphabet."

"Say what?"

"The alphabet. Recite it."

And just so I know I get catch. The question too easy. Too easy like a calm blue sea. And, pardner, I look at that sea and I think about Alicia and the warm soft curving sadness of her lips and her eyes full with crying, make me feel to cry for me and Alicia and Trinidad and America and I know like when you make a bet you see a certain card play that it will be a miracle if the card you bet on play. I lose, I know. But I is still a hero. I can't bluff forever. I have myself down as classy. And, really, I wasn't frighten for nothing, not for nothing, wasn't afraid of jail or of poverty or of Puerto Rico or America and I wasn't vex with the fellar who sell me the passport for the thousand dollars, nor with Iron Jaw and Squirrel Eyes. In fact, I kinda respect them. "A . . . B . . . C . . ." And Squirrel Eyes take out another cigarette and don't light it, just keep knocking it against the pack, Tock! Tock! Tock! K . . . L . . . M . . . And I feel I love Alicia . . . V . . . W . . . and I hear Paul Robeson sing "Old Man River" and I see Sammy Davis Jr. dance Mr. Bojangle's dance and I hear Nina Simone humming humming "Suzanne," and I love Alicia; and I hear Harry Belafonte's rasping call, *"Daay-o, Daaay-o! Daylight come and me* want to go home," and Aretha Franklin screaming screaming, "...Y ... Zed."

"Bastard!" the squirrel eyes cry out. "Got you!"

And straightaway from another door two police weighed down with all their keys and their handcuffs and their pistols and their nightstick and torchlight enter and clink their handcuffs on my hands. They catch me. God! And now, how to go? I think about getting on like an American, but I never see an American lose. I think about making a performance like the British, steady, stiff upper lip like Alec Guinness in *The Bridge on the River Kwai*, but with my hat and my boots and my piece of cigar, that didn't match, so I say I might as well take my losses like a West Indian, like a Trinidadian. I decide to sing. It was the classiest thing that ever pass through Puerto Rico airport, me with these handcuffs on, walking between these two police and singing,

Gonna take ma baby
Away on a trip
Gonna take ma baby
Yip yip yip
We gonna travel far
To New Orleans
Me and ma baby
Be digging the scene

PART III

Looking In

HINDSIGHT

BY ROBERT ANTONI

San Fernando

(Originally published in 1992)

B oy, let me give you a little story while we here, show-ing you just what kind of story this story you hearing has become. It was, I suppose, three or four years af-ter I'd arrive back from medical school in England. The little nurse comes running in to tell me, "Doctor, dey a oldman standing up outside dere, only rubbing up he bamsee groaning groaning like he sit down on a porcupinefish!" "Well," I tell her, "we better get him in here right away." So I ask the old-man to drop he drawers, and we put him to lie down quiet on the table with the pillow beneath he belly, and he blueblack bamsee standing up tall in the air in what we call the *jackknife position.* But before I go in from behind to take a look, I ask the oldman what is the problem. "Doctor," he says, "big big prob-lem. Ninety years I been shitting like a pelican, me mummy tell me, and dis never happen before." "Well," I ask again, "what is the problem?" He says he can't make a caca. "Every time I try, doctor, I feel one pain in me ass like I been feeding on groundglass, and thumbtacks, and fishhooks!"

So I take the proctoscope from out the cupboard, I grease it down liberally with the K-Y Jelly, and I ask the little nun-nurse to open up he cheeks fa me to push the proctoscope inside. But before I can get near him with this proctoscope, before I can even come close, the oldman seizes up he bamsee tight tight trembling, and he lets loose a bawl like a Warra-hoon spying a quenk: "Ay-ay-ay-ay-ay-ay!" Of course, I jump back quick like if it is *me* sit down on the porcupinefish now, and when the oldman's bamsee stops quivering, I ask him what is the matter. He says, "Doctor, I beg you, please don't push dat imperial cannon you holding up inside me. Not to say I too manmen to take little plugging in de softend like a buller. But doctor, contrary to de doctrines of history, contrary to de chronicles of all de schoolchildren's economics books, dis little black backside ain't big enough to accomodate de Royal Navy!"

Well, I have to smile a little bit at that one. I rub up the oldman's bamsee nice and gentle, and I promise him so long as he relax heself, I wouldn't give him no more pain. "But Mr. Adderly," I tell him, "if you don't let me push this ting inside there, how I ga look to find out what giving you all the groundglass, and thumbtacks, and fishhooks?" I tell him to turn he head and try to distract heself—think about a cricket match, or he girlfriend, or something so—and I promise him he wouldn't feel the cannon. Now I lubricate he bamseehole too with a squeeze of the K-Y Jelly to try to relax him, and now he tells me, "Doctor, I don't know what kind of ting you put-ting up inside me dere, all I can say it must be make from ice cream: cool, and soft, and lovely!"

Now I slide the proctoscope inside easy enough, I pump up the little bulb a few times to send some air inside there to inflate the mucosal folds, and I light up the little lightbulb at the end. But boy, when I bend down to take a look, when I focus my eye through this proctoscope, is now I feel the por-cupinefish: just there at the recto-sigmoid junction, where the third portion meets up with the sigmoid flexure (because the rectum is constructed in three divisions of 5 and 3 and

.5 inches in length, the first half curving towards the apex of the prostate gland shining in the middle, then backward and upward curving again on itself to culminate with the orifice of the fecal opening in the end, which is of course where all the caca comes out)—in others words, right there at the onset, in the very beginning, just there at the source of this oldman's rectum, I find an eyeball staring back at me cool cool like if I am the asshole looking out!

Of course this thing is impossible! It could never be! But the *harder* I look, the *surer* I am that is exactly what it is. And of course, when I nudge my nose at the proctoscope fa the little nurse to take a looksee, she only lets loose a cry, "Mother of Jesus!" and she bolts fa the door.

Of course, I excuse myself fa quick weewee and I bolt out the door behind her, I fire down a quick one, and when I get back I tell the oldman, "Mr. Adderly, I don't know how to put this ting any other way: you got a third eye inside there blinking at me, right up at the top of you asshole!"

Of course, the oldman gives me a face like I gone viekee-vie now fa true. But then he begins to chuckle little bit, he bamsee still standing up in the air giggling way. "Mr. Adderly," I tell him, "if you know a pretty joke you better give it to me quick, because just now I ga shit down this place with enough caca fa you and me together!"

"Doctor," he says, "dat eyeball you seeing not belonging to me a-tall. Even dough in truth I must be carrying it round a good long time. Dat eyeball belong to me daddy. You see, daddy used to wear dat eyeball make from glassbottle, and he used to take it out every night and leave it in a cup of water above de kitchen sink. De story goes dat one morning as a little boy, I climbed up on top de sink and I drank down de cup, eyeball and all. So, doctor, I suppose dat glassbottle eyeball must be rolling round me belly all these years, and it only now stick up on de way out. "

"Well," I tell him, "as they say, hindsight don't drive motorcar. And that is a good thing, because if you ever want to shit happy again, I ga have to remove it."

"Pluck it out!" he says. "Let me smell me way to Dover!"

"England?" I ask.

"No, doctor, Shakespeare. You play de Regan fa me old Grenada: is de plague of de times when madmen lead de blind!"

"Oh-ho," I say. "In that case, you better open up you earhole again fa me to pour in the poison."

Now I take the anuscope from out the cupboard, I grease it down too, and I replace it fa the proctoscope. I press down the lever to open up the two halves of the anuscope, I reach inside there with a long ring-forceps, and in no time a-tall I pluck it out. Of course, before I have a chance to remove the anuscope, before I even have a chance to brace meself: *Boodoomboom-doodoomdoom-boom-boom-boom!* And boy, dat ain't groundglass, it ain't thumbtacks, and it ain't fishhooks. It come out flowing easy as poetry!

UNCLE ZOLTAN

BY ISMITH KHAN

Central Market, Port of Spain

(Originally published in 1994)

The last time I saw Uncle Zoltan was in the Central Market in Port of Spain. He was still the hard tough man he had always been, barrel-chested, thick arms and legs to go with it, and now he was beginning to show a little paunch. His trousers were caught by a wide belt way down low, below the navel. But his gait was the same, his arms thrown out to the sides like a gorilla ready to pounce, or a wrestler pacing about in stances before he got a hold. I was sure that he could still take on four men at a time and throw them helter-skelter in different directions. I had seen him do just that when I was a boy in the old Britannia Bar, then he went back to his nip or rum, and muttered to himself, "A man can't even drink he rum in peace no more."

I had been away for several years and I wanted to see as many of my huge family as I could, but no one knew where Uncle Zoltan lived. When I asked my mother she simply said that he might very well be doing a stint in the Royal Gaol. She saw him on occasion, either on his way to jail, or on his way back. He always stopped in to tell Mother that he was going "up" or that he was "out," and since Mother's house was the meeting place in the city for all the relations from the hinterland, he would simply leave word with her, "just in case" he would add, never saying just what. Every six months or so he gathered up a few things: a straight razor, a pair of wooden-soled shoes, a pipe and a copy of a book called *She* which he thought was the greatest book ever written; he had read it hundreds of times but it still fascinated him. "Every time I read it I find something new in it," he had told me.

Although he rarely shaved when he was on the outside, he had learnt that one should look one's best in jail. "You have to make the turnkeys respect you, then they will know that you is a gentleman." The wooden-soled shoes he took along because he did not like to step on the damp floor of his cement cell, it was too cold, too much of a shock when he awoke in the mornings. And he took along a pipe although he always smoked cigarettes on the "outside." Why? "Every schoolboy know the answer to that one," he assured me. If you had cigarettes you had to offer them around, and he was not one to hide odds and ends from his cell-mates like others did. The pipe needed only to be filled and if anyone wanted a puff, that was all right, but he did not have to run through as much tobacco if he smoked a pipe instead of cigarettes. I once suggested to him that he was foregoing his own pleasure by not smoking cigarettes, which he adored, simply to avoid having to share them around, but he only laughed. "You think I is one to cut my nose to spoil my face?" he asked in a tone of injured pride, which left me with the feeling that I should not press him any further.

What looked like spite to others was his code of honour, and somewhere in his mind he saw something proud, beautiful and honourable in this code of his. The reason he went to jail periodically, for example, was because he and his wife had a "falling out" years ago and she took him to court to get support for herself and their small child. He reasoned that she had a rich father and that he could take care of them; his pride was injured when they actually filed papers and brought him before the magistrate, who did not see eye to eye with him and ordered him to pay up or go to jail. In those days he had a little establishment on Charlotte Street in which he pretended to make filigree jewellery. For the most part he hired a few boys who were part apprentices, part errand runners and part bar attenders for Uncle Zoltan and his cronies who argued all day long in his "shop." He managed to get people to apprentice their young boys to him, not because he was a fine craftsman, but on my father's reputation. Everyone knew that it was my father who was the real craftsman, yet somehow the parents of the apprentices no doubt felt that something must have rubbed off on my Uncle Zoltan if his brother was so well known. And Uncle Zoltan never felt that he was being dishonest. As soon as one of the boys became fairly proficient and began to demand more wages or treatment like a full professional, my Uncle Zoltan would give him a sharp clout on his head and send him home. "And tell you poopa I want to talk with him . . . to tell him what a worthless rogue he have for a son . . . ain't even begin to learn the trade and he want full salary . . . It only have one boss here . . . and that is me!"

It was at this point in time that the magistrate ordered him to pay support. He did away with his "shop," and with the few dollars left he idled about with his cronies until they decided to send him off to jail, where he adapted nicely. He got to know the turnkeys and since he was no ordinary thief he did not have to do hard labour breaking stones at the quarry like the other prisoners. His class of prisoners had all the light jobs and my Uncle Zoltan managed to get out of those as well.

His mind was made up about one thing, that his father-in-law should take care of things, that he would in the end wear them out and they would finally leave him alone to live his life the way he wanted to, and so he went to jail at regular intervals at first, then later on when his father-in-law began to weaken, Uncle Zoltan went to jail at less frequent intervals, and then finally, when he was getting his gear all set for jail, no policeman came to serve him with a summons. He was infuriated. He got shaved and dressed and went up to visit his wife and his in-laws and propositioned the old man this way: "I have a good friend who want to sell a lorry . . . if you put up the money for me to buy it, I will work and save you all of these court costs." The old man all but fainted. His body became rigid; he could not even move a limb to strike Uncle Zoltan, so great was his rage.

I felt that I really wanted to see Uncle Zoltan before I left for the States, but my mother would not hear of it. "You know how he done gone and spoil up the family name . . . Sometimes when people ask me, I have to tell them that he ain't belong to this family . . . that he is only a stranger . . . that Khan is a common name . . . and now you want to go up to the jail and let the whole world know that he is family?" Of course she was right, I thought. What right did I have to go up to the jail and let everyone know that we had a jail-bird in the family? I was there for a short visit, and then I would be off, while everyone else would have to bear the shame of it all, so I let it go at that.

After a couple of days during which my mother had been turning things over in her mind, she asked very casually if I had heard anything of Uncle Zoltan. She must have realised that I would find him on my own anyway and now she decided to help, but not without a certain amount of sighs, groans and complaints. "Well, we couldn't be the last to have a jail-bird in the family," she sighed. I thought of any number of things I had learnt in the States about criminals and crime and people, and society being partly responsible and any number of other things which would excuse Uncle Zoltan, but I also knew that this wasn't my mother's way. She had to lay a good ground-work of shame, humiliation and "think about us here after you leave in a couple of weeks," so I waited without saying anything. "You know that that rascal nearly killed me right here in this house four months ago?" My heart leapt, because even as a boy I had heard a rumour that Uncle had killed a man in one of the backwater villages. He was what was known as a "Bad-John" in all of the rum shops in the city, and if some weakling in the family got into an argument with someone he could not beat, he would threaten, "I have a cousin who is the worst Bad-John in Trinidad . . . better watch you mouth," and as soon as the stranger learnt that he was toying with a relation of Bad-John Zoltan, they would drop the argument.

My mother kept rattling the breakfast dishes in her special disgruntled movements. I think that she wanted me to come to Uncle Zoltan's rescue, but first she would tell me what a really worthless type he was and how could I defend him, etc. etc., only to end up with a "Very well then, go and find him . . . and remember, he is your father's brother, we don't have any jail-birds on *my* side of the family, thank God." Of course, I knew all of this about my mother, but she apparently knew me even better than I thought I knew her.

My instinctive reply was, "Did he really try to kill *you?*"

She took away another armful of dishes and came back adjusting her hair over her temples with the motions of an actress-philosopher who had set her own stage, who had fully prepared her audience, and now she had them tense with the "And then what happened?" kind of expectation which she had so thoroughly ingrained in all of us children since we were toddlers at her knees, listening to all of those gory tales of ancient Indian mythology. I had no sooner asked my foolish "And then what happened?" than I realised that I had played right into her hands. She remained silent, moving back and forth, not without a kind of triumph in her gait and strut, until I asked again, with the old childish image of Uncle Zoltan burying the corpse of a man somewhere in the hinterland. I was almost tempted to ask her whether he really did kill a man in the old days, but I checked myself. It was a foolish kind of exasperation I felt, and if my mother knew me well, I knew her well too. She would not speak her line until and unless she could sense just the right amount of exasperated curiosity in her listener's voice.

"Well, did he *really* try to kill you?" and for good measure I thought that I would add her own little refrain, "Right here in this house?"

She had one hand on her hip and a pot spoon in the other before she felt that she was quite ready to answer. "Well," she said, "you know what kind of man he is; I don't have to tell you." I let out a long sigh, cupping my forehead in my palm.

"Look, Ma . . ." I began, but she did not let me finish; it was her dream come true—both listener and audience were worked up to the point where something had to happen, as it did.

"Well . . . he didn't really try to kill me in the way you think."

"Oh," I let out, "thank God for that."

"But that ain't all . . . that ain't all," she said hastily, as though sensing that she was losing her ground, her audience, her flow and gentle build-up to crescendo.

"Well, what happened then?" I asked with even more exasperation than before. I must have stood up without realising it, and she was quick to take advantage of this and give herself another pause.

"Sit down and listen . . . why don't you. You're just like your father's side of the family . . . always getting excited over nothing."

I sat down, and I decided that I was not going to say another word . . . not a single word for the rest of my stay. I'd been too excitable—well, I wasn't going to be any longer, I would wait and wait and wait, and even if it took until doomsday, I would wait that long for her to tell her tale.

"Now listen," she said, sitting down now across from me, her pot spoon still in hand as she began, "your Uncle Zoltan come running in that yard (she pointed to the yard with her pot spoon) must be three four five month gone. You know how I like to sit down in the backyard under the breadfruit tree when it get hot by two o'clock?" I nodded. "Well, that boy (she always referred to Uncle Zoltan as *that boy*) come running into my yard like a deer out of season. He see me sitting in me rocker half asleep and he run come and bury he face in my lap. 'Oh God, Didi . . . I kill a man, and police after me.' Your father wasn't home at the time, otherwise I don't know *what* would happen. My heart jump! I ask him, 'Who you kill, boy, why . . . why?' But he only want me to hide him from the police. Well, what to do? I feel how he heart beating and how he shakin', so I ask him better he eat something before he faint in the hot sun. Mister man well eat and he well drink and just before five o'clock, you know, just before your father come home, he come and say to me, 'Didi, I don't want to bring shame on the family. I have to go to the bush and lay low . . . I have to lay low.'

"'Suppose they catch you and lock you up?' I ask he, and he only walkin' up and down, shaking he head as if he really don't know what to do. 'I have to go to the bush and lay low . . . lay low,' that is all he could say, and he walkin' up and down, up and down. I had to take one of my heart pills, my heart begin beating so hard too. 'Didi . . . you could lend me a couple dollars till next month, please God . . . I go pay you back, so help me God.' That is the exact exact words he say. Well, you know I so frighten, every noise I hear I think that is the police comin' to lock him up, and then it gettin' to be five o'clock, I say to myself, if you father come here and catch him, he will hand him over to the police . . . you know what kind of man your father is, I don't have to tell you . . . brother or no brother, if he really done gone and kill a man, you father will hand him over. Well anyway, to make a long story short, I have a few shillings save up from my market expenses and I give him five dollars. 'Listen, boy,' I say to him, 'if you really in trouble I feel glad that you come to one of the family instead you go to a perfect stranger.'"

She stopped to catch her breath, and I could sense all the old anger and the old fright of the moment rekindling in her veins. "Hm," she said, and as before I waited while she sat there in front of me, her pot spoon down at her side, her eyes staring blankly into space. "Well, is he a murderer now . . . ? In the old days he used to be just a pleasant jail-bird." She snapped out of her reverie. "That worthless rogue ain't kill nobody . . . he just did want to get a few dollars, and is me of all people that he choose to play this trick 'pon."

I felt that I would explode if I did not burst out in laughter, but I knew that I had to contain myself if she was going to help me to find Uncle Zoltan, and I could not help feeling the irony, the paradox of her emotions. Perhaps if Uncle Zoltan had killed a man she would feel better, at least her pride would not have been injured even if the family name was ruined. But as before, I thought to myself better not confront her with this thought.

"Anyway," she sighed, "blood thicker than water and I will feel bad if you have to go 'way without seein' your family on your father's side." My mother had thirteen brothers and three sisters. My father had only one brother, Uncle Zoltan, and as long as she could put Uncle Zoltan in that category of being on my father's side of the family, she was relieved. I could tell from the tone of her voice that a great change had come over her. "I made a few inquiries for you and I find out that he drivin' a lorry these days bringing fruits and ground provisions to the market from the bush . . . Don't ask me where he livin' because since that day he 'fraid to show he face in this house."

Did he finally persuade his father-in-law to get him that lorry? Did he really kill that man in the old days? Did he really get into trouble that day when he came to mother? From the way she told it, it seemed impossible to fake all that tense fear and anxiety unless he had really done something terrible.

The next morning I went to the Central Market. My mother had sent me to one of the vendors with whom Uncle Zoltan traded and I learnt he was due in from the bush that morning. I tried to find out from the man in the market any number of things about Uncle Zoltan, but I learnt nothing. "Your uncle is a funny kind of man . . . I don't have to tell you that. If anybody ask him any kind of question, he tell them to mind their own business, and you know what kind of Bad-John he is, so you leave him alone . . . Look, look . . . look, he comin' now."

I turned and saw the burly stocky man with his arms flung out to the sides like a gorilla, his beard and his hair of the same length. As he got closer I could see that the shoes he wore were made of old automobile tires and his trousers were three-quarter length, frayed at the bottom. And I could tell that he must have recognised me; he gave a little jump to one side and his head tipped forward as though he could not believe his own eyes. He threw his arms around me and then, with his powerful hands still on my shoulders, stood back at arms' length to get a better look at me.

"Boy, you don't know how you gettin' to look more like your father every day." He was being very vain, but subtly so; he too was the image of my father when he was shaved and dressed up, and I could tell that he was very proud of that. And turning me around and around so that he could examine my chest and shoulders, the shape of my head from behind, he said to the vendor, "This is my own blood, you know, my own flesh and blood, man!" The vendor only nodded as though this were a rare occasion when he saw my Uncle Zoltan reacting to anything as a human being.

"Listen, boy," he said to the vendor, "the lorry outside on George Street . . . better get a couple of your idlers to unload . . . I have to spend this time with my nephew who I ain't see for years." And then turning to me, "Come on, man, let we go and fire one in the rum shop." We were headed for the old Britannia Bar which I remembered well, and as we moved through the streets Uncle Zoltan's arms, still thrown out, would bang into people, but he moved along unconcerned. I knew that if anyone got banged by his elbows and wanted to take him up on it, he would be quite ready to put them in their place. A few people looked around as they got struck by his arms, but that was all. When we got to the Britannia with its sawdust and its smells of ancient kegs of rum, the bar attender left a little clique he was gossiping with and came rushing over to Uncle Zoltan. "I want you to meet my nephew, man . . . just come down from USA," and he ordered a nip of rum without taking his eyes off me.

"So how are things up there . . . plenty motor cars . . . plenty people?"

"Yes," I said, "it's a big country . . ."

"I hear that everything work by machine up there . . . You could go into a restaurant and put your money in hole and food come out?"

"Yes," I said, "there are places like that, and . . ." I had the feeling that he was getting tense and anxious about something and he simply wanted to get these preliminaries out of the way.

"Listen, boy . . . you make any money up there?" he finally asked, facing me squarely. I hardly knew what to say. I had a few hundred, and the exchange was about two-to-one so I felt rich and expansive. I nodded grandly. He suddenly changed his tone of voice; it was now tuned down to a whisper. The bar attender had placed our drinks on the counter and disappeared. Uncle Zoltan turned his head slowly and suspiciously around as if to make sure that he was out of earshot, and he must have caught my eyes and the curiosity in them, then he changed his tone again and became loud. He raised his glass filled with the amber rum, and not exactly proposing a toast to both of us but more a toast to the tall glass of rum which he had poured himself, he pronounced wildly, "Here's to those that wish us well . . . may the rest of them be damned in hell." I hardly had my glass to my lips when Uncle Zoltan poured the powerful rum down his gullet and wiped his mouth with the back of his hands. His body gave a quick little shiver as though his organism was jolted by the sudden impact of a crude blow, and then he smiled broadly and clapped his hand on my shoulder. "Picture of your father, boy . . . you is the picture of your father . . . it make me happy to see that you don't look like the other side of the family."

I suddenly thought all over again how strange life was. My father, who was older than Uncle Zoltan, treated him with a kind of firm, strict, clipped tone—it was often one of admonition—and for the first time in my life I realised that if Uncle Zoltan feared no one or respected no one else in this world, not even God, he was afraid of my father. He was always docile and fawning whenever he spoke to my father, or rather when my father spoke to him, because it was always a stern kind of lecturing to Uncle Zoltan—how he should mend his ways, how my father had heard through the grapevine what a low type he was, how little ambition he had, etc. etc. . . . And Uncle Zoltan, in his own way and in his own world, treated all the people he came in contact with with the same kind of harsh clipped words of condemnation for which they all respected him. I was a little surprised to find that he was reacting to me in pretty much the same way that he reacted to my father, and I wondered if he sensed this. He had poured a second shot as tall as the first, but now he was savouring it. He sipped this one slowly and he began to get all furtive and cagey; each time he had a sip of rum he looked over his shoulder to make sure that he was not being watched or followed or overheard. He also developed a sudden twitch of the arm with each sip of rum as though he were warding off a sudden blow; his eyes would twitch and again he would turn his head around ever so slowly. I thought that any moment now he would come right out and ask me whether anyone was listening to us or staring at us, but he didn't, he only became more and more agitated.

"Listen, man . . ." he finally said, "I am in a jam!"

"What kind of jam?" I asked.

He took another sip of rum and clenched his teeth together. The bar attender came strolling along to see if there was anything we needed and Uncle Zoltan again changed his tone. He slapped me on the shoulder, grasped me by the shoulder and literally rocked me back and forth.

"So, man . . . what you doin' up there in the USA?" And not being able to answer his question as quickly as he was ready with another, he went on again. "Listen, man . . . I want you to carry a message for me when you go back to the USA. It have a fellar who write a book called *She*. I want you to tell him that I read it and is the biggest book I ever read . . . You think that you could carry this message for me?"

I nodded half-heartedly. I had the impression that the book was written by an Englishman and that he was no longer alive, nor had he ever lived in the States, and I also wondered just where and how one would go about finding such a person. Uncle Zoltan made it sound as though any place in the world was after all not too different from Trinidad and all one had to do was ask around. Just as I had found him, surely I could get word from the grapevine of anyone's whereabouts.

"I'll tell him," I said. I thought that the rum was going to my head too. The heat was unbearable; I had become spoilt by a temperate climate, air-conditioned movies where you could escape the worst of the summer, and at least the water in the taps of the most wretched tenements in New York was cold if you needed a drink. Everything died fast in the tropics, not just human bodies, but plants and insects and woodlice and mosquitoes. They all had their glorious colourful fling for a day, but the heat never let up and the water in the tap never cooled off and the frenzy of life was like a wound-up toy; it flirted, flitted and paraded in its glorious colours and then it died fast, and whether it was the weather or the rum, I thought about how simple it would be to go to the New York Public Library, look up something like a writers directory, find the man who wrote *She*, call him up on the phone and say,

"Look . . . I've just come back from Trinidad and I ran into this uncle of mine who leads one of the most isolated and curious kind of lives, and he has read your book and he wanted me simply to get in touch with you and tell you what a wonderful book you've written and how much it has done for his life."

But as soon as the bar attender looked at our drinks and was sure that we did not need anything else and wandered away, Uncle Zoltan changed his tone again. He was once more furtive and suspicious as though every word he had to say was to be in total secrecy. He took a sip of rum, gargled it about in his mouth, and clamped his eyes shut as he swallowed hard. "You come at the right time, man . . . it look as if my guardian angel send you." Just as he had scrutinised me in the market, I now looked carefully at him; he seemed a little bit older, his teeth were blacker than I had remembered and he had a small bump on his forehead just below the hair line, no doubt from butting someone with his head. I remembered how he fought—hands, feet, head—all came into play automatically. I could never understand how he managed to keep that finely shaped nose of his after the innumerable brawls he had been in.

He still looked over his shoulder from time to time to make sure that no one was listening, and his arm jerked in the same short spasms as if he was instinctively warding off blows from an unseen opponent. He must have noticed my concern and he pointed to the bump on his head. "You know how I get this?" he asked, but it was more of a statement than a question; he simply nodded as though there was some tacit understanding between us, a secret which we both knew, and although he did not explain, it was to be part of an even deeper and darker secret which came moments later. He grabbed me by the shoulder and drew me close to him so that he could almost whisper in my ear. "Listen, man . . . I need a few dollars."

I reached for my billfold, and he craned his neck again to make sure no one was watching, then he peered at the bills as I opened it up. "About how much do you need . . . what kind of jam are you in?"

"Man . . ." he shook his head with such pathos and regret, "this is just between you and me . . . I hope that you don't mention a word to the family . . . you know how they like to worry about things." I nodded, waiting with the open billfold in my hand to hear how much he thought he needed, but he simply said, "I leave it up to you . . . Whatever you can spare." He must have seen the question on my face. I didn't know what kind of jam he was in or how much I should give him. He finally drew me close to him and grated out in tense whispers, "I kill a man . . ." He stood me at arms' length to examine the shock on my face. "I kill a man and police after me. I have to go to the bush and lay low . . . lay low!"

After I gave him a five, and watched him leave the Britannia Bar, he turned once to say, "Just between you and me . . . Remember, not a word to the family."

And I waved out to him as he disappeared in the crowds of the market shoppers.

TOWN OF TEARS

BY ELIZABETH NUNEZ

Laventille

(Originally published in 2000)

Laventille, home of the shrine of Our Lady of Fatima, town of tears. *Laventville*, the poet once called it: *To go downhill / from here was to ascend.* He would not be wrong. Yet to go uphill was also to ascend, to reach such splendor it blinded the eye. For there, at the top, the sun gilded the roofs of the shrine and the tiny blue and white chapel next to it and made the blue of the blue sky bluer and the white of the white clouds whiter. And if one looked up, as always one was compelled to do, one followed the dazzling arc of the sky to a sea shimmering gold and silver on clear days, gray and still magnificent when it rained.

One saw this from the top of Laventille, though one knew there was more: after the grassy green savannah for horse racing and polo, and men in flannel trousers playing cricket, and after the gardens for ladies strolling arm in arm along pathways lined with lilies and orchids, and after the white picket–fenced bandstand for brass-buttoned police serenading young lovers, and after the governor's white house and the other mansions (the archbishop's castle, the cathedrals, the prime minister's quarters, the sprawling villas of the merchants), after those palatial homes of the rich, and the more modest, yet assertive houses of the middle class, there would come the others—the cement hovels of the poor—staggering up the hill like drunks stumbling over choked gutters, stray dogs and half-naked children. *Five to a room*, the poet said. Looking back, *the hot, corrugated iron sea.*

There, on the Sunday before Zuela and Rosa were to make their pilgrimages to Our Lady, on the very day a fisherman found himself the center of attention in Otahiti, the body of another woman was discovered. Black, poor, and therefore of no consequence, her disappearance had not made news in *The Guardian*, where no one expected it would, but neither did it make news in the streets nor in the rum shops, nor in the backyards where gossip was rife. Shame and envy had silenced tongues (they said two brothers had loved her and she had had them both)—silenced tongues, that is, until two pigs vomited on a dirt road in Laventille, two spike-haired black pigs caked with dried mud, fattening themselves on the remains of something that had once been alive and breathing—a carcass chopped into tiny bits and mingled with the food in their troughs, with the remains of dasheen, cassava, yam and rotting potatoes.

A young girl identified her first, pointing to an eyeball gleaming between the pink chunks of undigested food. "Melda. Is Melda self."

"No body, no crime," Boysie was heard to have said months before. No body, no murder. No murder, no execution.

His henchmen laughed in the judge's face when they released Boysie from Death Row.

Then someone spotted the chewed-off finger of a woman. Weeks later, a man no longer able to contain his grief claimed the ring she wore. "Melda. Is Melda self. I self give her that ring." *Not the brothers.*

That same week, two hearts still moist with blood were found on top of the garbage dump in the La Basse. The vultures froze in midair and then dove like bombers. In the days that followed, ten more women caught the spirit and set up shop in that town of tears. People poured out of the valley on the feast day of Our Lady—Rosa and Zuela, too—for two women said they saw Our Lady come down in a circle of bright light over the shrine of Fatima near the little chapel on the top of the Laventille hill. Our Lady here to protect them! And the priest did not dispute that, nor did he chase away the hundreds who followed to light votive candles and put coins down the slit in the tiny box he had ingeniously placed at the feet of Our Lady.

Zuela and Rosa had given money, too, but not because they were terrified by two hearts for racehorses found throbbing in the La Basse, or because two pigs had vomited the remains of a black woman chopped into fodder, or because fish had eaten the eyeballs of a white woman and gouged out her lips and tongue, but because they needed Our Lady to work her miracle on them, too, to visit them, too, to push back to the darkness a thought that now tormented them, that now gave them no peace.

It was Rosa who would bring them together, Rosa who would remember and would rekindle between them a friendship that would change what was left of her life forever, though time had seemingly calcified to stone that terrible moment she had shared with Zuela behind the hibiscus bush. Yet it was mere chance that caused her to meet Zuela again. She never would have seen her were her soul not so tormented by remorse, yet uplifted by a sort of perverse satisfaction for the thing she had not yet done. Rosa would have missed her completely were she not so terrified, and yet morbidly elated, by the possibility of doing it; if, not so frightened by this wrestling of good and evil within her, she had not sought to shut out all distraction from Our Lady, who could help her; if she had not thus forced herself into deep meditation of another mystery of the rosary; if she had not drawn her black mantilla down the sides of her face, hoodlike, so she did not see Our Lady's devotees part to the edges of the dirt road; she did not hear the thunder of footsteps racing behind her; she did not jump out of the way before the gaggle of uniformed schoolchildren tumbled her to the ground. Even then she might not have no-ticed the woman who stooped to help her out of the bramble of bushes. Jarred forcibly out of the Sorrowful mystery of the rosary, she might not have noticed if, in that instant, she had not looked up and her eyes had not caught in the eyes of the other woman, a sadness deep, penetrating, familiar, that sent her head whirling:

One little girl.

A string of pearls.

A man with a pole.

Another little girl, her eyes as sad as a woman's. A girl. A woman-child, swishing her hips and laughing. "That is noth-ing. I see that already. Chinaman do that to me already."

She bolted to her feet but the woman was gone. She squeezed her eyes shut and other pictures came—distorted, blurred, hazy. Terrifying. She fought to focus them but they slipped rapidly in and out of her mind, eluding her. Frantically, she searched for the woman, desperate to stop the collision of images now falling one on top of the other—two, three, five, seven at a time. Disturbing. Unnerving. A memory? A past? She shoved her way through the masses of sweaty bod-ies thronging up the hill, pursued by that one split second of recognition, clear, precise, and sharp. Unmistakable. She had seen those eyes before; she had known that face well once before. *Daughter. Daughter.* The sound clear as a bell resounded in her ears. *Daughter. Daughter.* Her child's voice calling.

The sharp points of the stones along the muddied dirt road penetrated the soles of her shoes and bruised the bottoms of her feet, but she took no notice of the pain, nor of the women—their heavy bosoms drooping low over their swollen bellies, their arms lost in white suds trailing down the sides of their washtubs—who looked up when she passed, a hardness around their mouths that should have stopped her, but did not, nor of the half-naked children in tattered undershirts who streamed out of one-room houses to taunt the nuns: "Hail Mary, holy white ladies. Full of grace, holy white ladies." She barely heard them. Nor did she notice the stone-still men standing before the doorway of their houses, legs apart, arms folded militantly across naked chests turned tar black in the sun. She did not see these people from that town of tears who knew already that the rush upstream left nothing but rubble in its wake when it rolled back down again; who were certain that two brothers, fighting over a ring on the decaying finger of the body of the woman that two pigs had disgorged, were not the ones who had chopped her into fodder. For the people in that town had no doubt that such diabolical barbarity could originate only from the valley below.

Everything was obscured in that tangle of photographs in Rosa's mind. Screened out, too, was the blaze that had sent her racing to Our Lady for her cooling waters: her fear of vengeance on Cedric, which was lost now in that sudden clearing to a past she had made herself forget. *Daughter. Daughter.* A tiny girl with skin as brown as sand. Through the wild hibiscus they had seen . . . *Daughter.* A little girl who lived with the woman who came on Fridays to iron clothes for her mother on the Orange Grove estate. A little girl who told her, "That is nothing. I see that already. Chinaman do that to me already."

At the top of the hill she saw her, her faded yellow cotton dress tight against a belly that rose, round as a watermelon, beneath her tiny breasts, her long black hair pulled back from her copper-brown face, her eyes staring steadily in her direction, questioning, doubting. She stood on the hill, apart from the crowd, framed by a sky indigo and magnificent, which plunged headily downward to where speedboats splayed frothy long white lines like sunrays across a glistening sea.

"Daughter?"

The woman squinted against the blinding sunlight.

"Daughter!" Rosa called out to her again, certain now. But the woman frowned, stepped back, and disappeared into a new wave of bodies crashing on the crest of the hill.

Daughter. Daughter. Again she gave voice to the name and the sound came back on her ears and unlocked the memories.

They had pressed their faces into the hibiscus bush, she and the little girl. Yet long after the girl had turned away, she still remained, her cheeks bleeding where the sharp ends of the dried twigs had made welts down the sides of her face, her eyes snapping photographs. Click! Click!

The little girl tugged her dress to force her away from the bushes, but she resisted. Click, click. Each detail was meticulously captured, each image indelibly imprinted. Click, click!

The little girl tugged again. She fought her. The petals from red hibiscus fell from thin branches and turned blue in the dirt. Click, click! The little girl laughed. "That is nothing. I see that already."

Then the world went still: "Chinaman do that to me already. Chinaman done do that to me."

Memory fused to stone and was sealed off in the horror of that possibility, sealed off until the pictures returned years later with Cedric, she sprawled on the dining room floor, panties clinging to one ankle, the ends of her skirt to her throat, Cedric thrusting, the smile on his lips indistinguishable from the smirk on the mouth of the man behind the hibiscus bush, his words the same as that man's: *Beg. Beg. You like it so. You like it so. Beg.* Then a truth more horrible confronted her, one that connected the child Rosa, her face sunk into broken ends of the hibiscus bush, to the woman Rosa, dazed by an incomprehensible sense of betrayal when Cedric demanded again: "Beg. Beg for it, white lady."

In the confessional, the priest said the pictures she saw that night did not come from memory but, rather, from a sinful imagination, planted there by Satan. None of what she saw had happened—not the man with the pole, not the girl with the pearls, not her friend, swinging her hips like a woman, laughing: "Chinaman done do that to me already." And she loosened the connection in nine days of rosaries to the Blessed Mother, buried Daughter, the child now a woman called Zuela, in a righteous resentment of Cedric three years deep.

Now, near the tops of the gru-gru boeuf trees that rose from the squalor of raw cement bricks pushing up the hill to the shrine of Our Lady, Rosa saw her again. She turned when Rosa touched her shoulders and called her Daughter, her eyes calm with recognition.

"You. It's really you." But she would say no more. "Not now," she said. "Not here in Laventille."

"When?" Rosa pressed her. "I must speak to you. *Must.*" She stretched our her hand, feverish with desperation, but Zuela pulled hers away.

"Not now."

"When?"

Zuela heard the hysteria in her voice, but it did not startle her. She, too, had removed the boulder damming her memory. "After the Benediction," she said, and turned toward the steps of the chapel where the priest had just emerged from behind the acolytes holding the gilded monstrance high above his head, his hands draped by the white shawl that covered his shoulders.

"Later," she whispered.

It was not enough for Rosa. "I won't find you."

The woman she had called Daughter studied her face. No part of her moved, only her eyes boring deeper and deeper into Rosa's as she peeled away layers to the past. "Rosa." She whispered her name.

"You'll get lost." Rosa's eyes brimmed water. "I won't be able to find you again." She reached for her hand.

Zuela frowned and pursed her lips, but she did not pull away her hand. To Rosa it seemed she stayed that way for an eternity, but suddenly she sighed, a long outpouring of her breath that seemed to empty her body of air. The sound, streaming through her lips, reverberated hollow in the cavity of her chest. "Since last I see you, I live with Chinaman." She breathed in again. "In Nelson Street." Her eyes were hard but there was a softness in her voice when she spoke, the hardness directed to something or someone Rosa could not see, the softness to Rosa. "Come see me there."

The acolytes had reached close to them and were moving in the direction of the shrine nestled just a few feet to the left of where they stood. Clouds of incense wafted from their censers and thickened the air. In the torpid heat of the afternoon, made more intense by the sweet smell of ripe mango and gru-gru boeuf and the stink of human sweat and animal excrement, the pungent odor of the incense plunged into nostrils and worked its hypnotic spell. The crowd surged forward and burst into a hymn to Our Lady, pulling Zuela and Rosa in its tow. Rosa reached for the skinny branch of a bush sprouting stubbornly through a space in the gravel-stoned pathway, and anchored herself to the ground, but when she looked up, she saw Zuela drowning helplessly in the folds of that speckled sea.

She felt cheated, robbed of her chance for the answers she was frantic to find and yet not find, that she believed were there behind the screen that had begun to part on Zuela's face. Yet before the afternoon would end she would lose this frenzied urgency to talk to Zuela, and she would wait the week it took for Cedric to send her flying like a madwoman to the Chinaman's shop in Nelson Street. For out of the dark despair that enveloped her then, came an epiphany. It left her dazed, burning, smoldering in the brilliance of its searing clarity as it must have left those who bad witnessed the Vision, Our Lady descending in a blaze of light: she had had her miracle. Our Lady had made one for her in Laventille. Her revelation. And at that moment she understood, in a way denied to her before, why the little girl could not pry her off the hibiscus, why she still pressed her face into its branches though its sharp ends tore her cheeks.

For then, above the silence that descended on the crowd below the drone of the priest now chanting his prayers in Latin; beyond the shouts that followed "Alleluia!" when he raised the monstrance, the Body of Christ gleaming white from the center, radiating metal rays of gold, Rosa unraveled the threads of the knot that had tied her to Cedric, Cedric to the man behind the hibiscus bush, Cedric to the man the little girl thought no different from the Chinaman: *He do that to me, too, already. He done do that.*

How could her mother have known how desperately

she needed Cedric? She herself had not known. Not in the way Our Lady's miracle would make it known to her. When she said yes to Cedric after he asked her to marry him, she thought she was giving him what she was certain he craved, what the man behind the hibiscus craved, though she did not remember him then, only the feelings: awe for the power the girl held over him, and pity for the man made savage by his hunger for her. They were feelings that filled her with such shame for having them that they detached themselves from the reality she had witnessed and sank deep past her memory. Then all that remained was the awe, and, later, the pity that surfaced with Cedric.

When she was desperate for respite from the rubbing of flesh against the hardness of her mattress and Cedric walked past her house, dark and curly haired, the fabric of his pants so cheap and old it clung to his legs, she thought: Here was a safe place for her passions. Here was the son of a woman who scaled fish on a beach with a pan full of bloody fish guts anchored between her gnarled knees. Here was a man who did not know his father, who would not acknowledge him even if he knew him, so certain she was that he was fathered by one of the toothless men, still not old, threading twine through the loops of torn seine strung between bamboo poles, swigging mouthfuls of raw cane rum to deaden the pain of twisted limbs and wounds still fresh from their fight with the sea.

No, Cedric could not have dreamed a woman like her would say *Yes*, in spite of the Latin and Greek he read. Yes, in spite of the baccalaureate degree he would get from a university in London. He was ripe for awe of her. She could relieve her passion, surrender it to him and still keep her power. So she thought.

Then he said: "Beg. Beg for it, white lady."

Though she began to despise him, she pitied him, too, because it was she, not he, who held the power. It was she who bent his knees, like the white woman in Otahiti who drove an Indian farmer's son mad with his obsession to own her, though he was a doctor and had long since left his tomato patch.

Now Zuela had broken the lock on the vault where she had sealed off her memory of the photographs. Now she saw them clearly. Not even the tremulous shouts of a crowd hopeful for the appearance of Our Lady here and now in Laventille, nor the chants of the blue-frocked acolytes too young yet to need Our Lady's miracles, could dim those pictures now vivid before her eyes. Frame by frame she retrieved them, each one impeccably preserved, each one fresh, shining, precisely detailed as if she had taken it yesterday, printed it today.

A *girl*.

A girl younger than either she or the girl she called Daughter, now Zuela.

A girl no more than nine years old, in a pink sleeveless dress.

A girl in a pink sleeveless dress, straight black hair hanging long past her shoulders, bangs across her forehead.

A *girl*.

A little girl in a pink sleeveless dress with bangs across her forehead. Big, bright eyes.

A little girl with red lipstick on her mouth and rouge on her cheeks, a string of pearls tumbling down her flat chest.

A little girl, no more than ten, younger than either she or Daughter, now called Zuela.

A *child*.

A child in high-heeled shoes, red lipstick on her mouth.

A *man*.

A man old as her father, old enough to be the girl-child's father.

A man with dark brown skin, browner than a sapodilla's, browner than the girl-child's brown skin.

A *man*.

A man in long black pants and a sleeveless white undershirt.

A man, his fingers on his waist.

A man with long black pants, with his fingers on the buckle of his belt on his waist.

A man old enough to be the girl-child's father.

A man with hairy hands, his fingers on the zipper of his pants.

A *pole*.

A man with a pole.

Say you want it. Say you want it now or I beat you. Say you want it or I beat you. Beg! Beg!

A man old enough to be the girl-child's father.

On his knees now.

Please. Please beg. Beg, please.

A man with a pole begging. A little girl in a pale pink dress, a string of white pearls.

THE VAGRANT AT THE GATE

BY Wayne Brown

Woodbrook

(Originally published in 2000)

Bad news: the 626 abruptly decelerating, all power gone, in a stressed and disappointed silence. But then, good news: an acquaintance in a white Galante had been behind me all along and now obligingly stopped too. ("Pull the hood.") His brief and hesitant self-insertion therein proved—as we'd both expected, though I still hoped—infertile. He left to go in search of his mechanic, "an electrics guy" from upper St. James.

I'd pulled over to the curb facing south on X, two or three car lengths above Y. (X: a north-south residential Woodbrook street. Y: one of the main roads crossing it.) It was not yet nine, but already there was only one viable pool of shade left on the pavement. It came from the dormer-window protrusion of an old forties Woodbrook house which had been expensively and hideously "modernized." I retired into it to wait.

Almost at once, the vagrant materialized. I glanced at him irritably.

He was your standard vagrant: matted hair, too-bright eyes, red skin upon which the passionate sun had laid a light gloss of washed black, like an old j'ouvert greasing. Baggy trousers, still recognizably khaki, curling outward at the waist like the lip of a vase, from which rose the stem of his tucked-in torso, with its furious navel.

"Eh, uncle, uh beggin' you," etc.

The way he said it, it sounded rehearsed: not quite your true-blue vagrant's heartfelt expression of illimitable desperation. And the light in his eyes was not quite ownerless, I saw: not quite the unsigned light of lunacy. But what to do. My pocketful of coins changed hands ("T'ank you, boss!") and he was turning away when the oblong bulge in my shirt pocket caught his attention. He ducked and peered at it, making a vagrant's urgent mime—two forked fingers tensely pumping from his lips—and I gave him the Benson and lit it for him, doing this with a look which told him we both knew he was pushing the envelope.

For a moment, inhaling, he was all concentration. Then: "Heh-heh-heh," he said sheepishly into his chest, turning away.

He didn't go very far. There was an electricity pole not far from the corner, a car length or so south of the 626, and he went and leaned on it in the immemorial posture of a whore: hand cupping elbow, cigarette at the ready, one bare sole cocked against the pole.

And, five years ago, I might have rounded on him ("Haul y'ass! What the fock more you want? G'won, move!"). But I discovered I didn't have that part anymore—or at least, didn't have it that morning—and so I lit one myself, and paced irritably back and forth in the little pen of shade by the 626's boot, and presently fell to considering the house across the street, to which my attention had been drawn by the sound of a car engine being laboriously tumbled . . . and then wailingly revved . . . until, with a few last, precautionary, throat-clearing revs, the car itself was modestly induced to demit its driveway—or so I deduced, since both were out of sight on the far side of the house.

On my side there wasn't much to see. Chain link between unpainted concrete pillars, backed by a tall, untidy hedge and bisected by a padlocked garden gate, BRC on steel pipe, from which a flagging flagstone path led almost at once to four or five concrete steps with, at their summit, an empty, small verandah and a door through whose half-height panes of glass the morning sun irradiated confusedly. The place had a neglected, impoverished look. The galvanized zinc roof was rusting badly.

From twenty feet away: "Watch dis," the vagrant said. He might have been speaking to himself.

In the house behind me, the "modernized" house, a glass sliding door opened, then closed, and a big, paunchy, Portugee man in perhaps his late forties came down the steps and out onto the pavement. He was evidently dressed for work: white short-sleeved shirt (pulling tight at the waist) with an under-vest showing; dark trousers. Big forearms, the hair on them long and black; the hair on his head, too, suspiciously black. He crossed behind the 626, close enough that a passing nod at its owner would have been natural. But he merely glanced angrily from the car to my face, and went on over. At the pad-locked gate he looked up and down the street, then banged the metal saddle three times.

"Um bad!" the vagrant wailed softly (the Michael Jackson song). "Um ba-ad!" And he pinched the stub of the cigarette, inhaled mightily, and blew the smoke up, straight up, to the bright blue morning sky.

In the house across the street the glass-paned door opened, and a woman—a youngish, brown-skinned woman in a housecoat of fading flowers with her hair in curlers—emerged and came down the steps to the garden gate. She might have been in her mid-thirties, or she might have been younger, for her face had the graven, naked-sad look of one not long come from sleep, and her gaze when she glanced across the street (at me, then at the vagrant) was appraising rather than disapproving. She and the Portugee man stood at the gate talking.

How is it that one can unerringly tell from forty feet away when a man and woman are talking about "doing it"?

Maybe it's just that they stand too close—even when separated by a BRC gate. Or maybe it's the way they take turns glancing around, though not as if expecting to see anyone. Or the sense you get, though out of earshot, that they are talking softly yet urgently . . .

At any rate, the woman seemed of a mind to demur (perhaps, I thought, because of the presence of two witnesses across the street). But the Portugee man's broad, white-shirted back gave off the uncompromising "planted" air of someone who was not about to move; and abruptly the woman broke away and went up the steps into the house and returned with a bunch of keys and opened the gate.

Locking it after him, she glanced a last time at the vagrant— and I saw that the vagrant had gone perfectly still. Then she turned and went up and in, closing the door behind her.

"Um baaad," the vagrant crooned softly, as though to himself. "Um ba-ad!" Abruptly he sang it out, harsh and loud: "Um baad! Um baaaad!"—and I turned, then said angrily: "Hey!"

The vagrant had slipped his hand into his trousers-front, and—staring hard at the house—was vigorously agitating himself there.

"Hey, *you*!" I shouted enraged, and the vagrant swung away, interposing his shoulder between me and what he was doing, and went on doing it.

I said, *"Jesus Christ!"* and swung away myself, and started walking—and in this way found myself abreast of the driveway of the "modernized" house from which the Portugee man had come. There was a car parked in it, some way in, near where the back steps would be. It was a silver shining Mercedes 300 SL: PBA something or the other.

And, writing this now, I cannot explain it, but I looked at that car and knew—knew—that what was taking place in the house across the street, the house with the once-more-locked garden gate, was not at all what I'd assumed it to be—not a solitary man's heat and hunger calling into some stifled night of marital loneliness (though I understood that the wailing, revving car, laboriously leaving from the far side of the house, had been the signal the Portugee man had been listening for); not a free negotiation between loins and heart, impassioned, urgent, yet free; not male want calling to female bewilderment— but the brute operation of money upon moneylessness (those broken flagstones, that neglected verandah, that badly rusting roof!), the adamantine imposition of power upon powerlessness and need.

Behind my back: "Um baad!" bellowed the vagrant suddenly. "Um ba-ad!" And I turned and saw that—hand out of sight, trousers-front shaking violently—he was glaring at the shut, glass-paned door of the shabby old forties Woodbrook house across the street—glaring at it as if he could kill it.

2.

It was minutes past nine, and though the street where the 626, without warning, had crossed over from life into death (and now lay by the curb, embalmed in silence) was a quiet, residential Woodbrook street, cars still came down it, one by one. I stared at each briefly but hungrily—for who wants to stand in the burning sun not fifty feet away from a violently masturbating vagrant?—but none was a white Galante that might be bearing my acquaintance and his "electrics guy." So, gloomily, I watched each car come, decelerating as it passed, and then of necessity—just as it came abreast of the engrossed vagrant—braking for the major road ahead.

("Um baaad!" bellowed the vagrant at sporadic intervals, glaring at the glass-paned door across the street, one hand working wildly in his trousers-front.)

Like that, there came down the road:

1) A dark blue Sonata driven by a young Syrian woman who, when she saw what she was pulling up next to, accelerated so desperately that she swung onto the major road barely ahead of a thundering garbage truck, which repaid her by shattering the quiet morning with a three-second blast of its horn.

2) A brown PAY Laser, piloted by a young creole tess who shook his head when he saw what he saw, bending over in such exaggerated disbelief or misapplied mirth that his forehead bumped his horn and made him jump.

3) A pastel Laurel, the padded cell of a well-dressed, middle-aged, red-skinned lady, who must have suffered terribly—or so the back of her head seemed to say—while she waited for a gap to open in the main road traffic, and who was full of hatred by the time it did, judging by the vengefully accelerating swerve with which she put behind her forever (except, perhaps, in her dreams) the lit and dreadful apparition suffusing her peripheral vision for a petrified Eternity.

None of these fazed the vagrant in the least.

("Um baad!" bellowed the vagrant at the house with the two unseen occupants and the locked garden gate. "Um baaaad!!!")

On the other hand, not even he could have ignored the battered pickup with three Indian guys wedged in front and a fourth with a power mower in the tray.

"Yuh crazy nigger!"

"Yuh nasty bitch!"

"Stay right dey, we bringin' de police for yuh mod-ah cont!"

The vagrant's hand stayed in his trousers but stopped moving. The guy in the tray jumped up and with an oath flung a cardboard box at him. (It missed.) Reflexively the vagrant picked it up, looked inside, then tossed it away into the gutter. With a chorus of obscenities the pickup turned onto the main road and was gone.

The vagrant looked dismayed. He glanced around him (including at me) disappointedly. And I was just judging it safe to return to my pool of shade, two car lengths or so from where he stood, when his gaze fell again on the glass-paned door, and I saw it strengthen there, and grip, and his hand slipped back into his trousers-front; and I said to myself with feeling, "Oh, *fuck!*" and for the *nth* time looked up the street in vain for the Galante.

(And if some amateur psychologist wishes to explain to me at this point that my reluctance to stand near the vagrant in that state was due to latent homosexual tendencies on my part, fine. I only know there's a certain, irrefragable distance from a masturbating man within which I am not prepared to stand; and the only pool of shade on the pavement lay well within it.)

"Um bad," the vagrant said pensively; and I saw that with him the trousers-front business was now meditative rather than frenetic.

Here a black PBB Corolla with dark-tinted windows came

down the street, pulled up for the major road, and stopped. There was a lull in the main road traffic, but the Corolla didn't move . . . a stream of cars passed by, then another lull . . . still the Corolla didn't move. And I had just amazed myself with a surge of fury, which for a moment actually had me looking around for a stone to pelt at it, when the vagrant threw himself upon it, screaming, "Uh go kill you! Uh go kill you!" kicking and banging on the fender and boot, and the black car leapt away like a startled animal, out onto the main road, and was gone.

"Uh go kill him!" the vagrant screamed, and his eyes were terrible. "Uh go kill him!"

Our eyes met. I nodded, and the vagrant saw, and his wildness abated slightly.

"Uh go kill him!" he shouted at me a third time, as if making sure I'd heard him right.

And I said, quite loudly (returning to my patch of shade at last), "Yeah, kill him. Kill his ass!"

"Uh go kill his mo-dah'ss," the vagrant said with desolate satisfaction. And he leaned on the telegraph pole and folded his arms and resumed watching the glass-paned door across the street, but without frenzy now.

And so we stood there, me and the interrupted vagrant, and watched the silent house across the street (in which, for some reason—though I claim a robust imagination and am no especial prude—I could only imagine what was taking place in there as occurring in the (foully named!) "missionary position," with the brown-skinned young woman almost out of sight and struggling to breathe beneath a great pale threshing bulk.)

And, sure enough, presently the glass-paned door opened and the Portugee man came out, dressed for work just as before, with behind him the young woman, barefooted now and wearing only an old thigh-length white T-shirt, imprinted with some fading festive scene.

She was in the process of taking the last curler out of her hair. (And that, for some reason, depressed me even more. To think he hadn't minded her keeping the curlers in!) She deposited it on the verandah sill and came down the steps and unlocked the garden gate and let him out.

"Uh-go-kill-his-mo-dah'ss," the vagrant said.

But he said it experimentally, in the tone of one rehearsing a phone number; and I knew that nothing was going to happen.

The Portugee man never looked at him. As he had done earlier, he glanced from my car to me (but without anger, now) and went on down his driveway and got straight into the Mercedes and started it and backed out and drove off, stopping for the major road, then going on. And I marvelled at his doing all that as if nothing at all had just happened: as if he were just a normal guy, driving off to work on a normal weekday morning.

The young woman in the T-shirt had stayed at the garden gate: presumably, I thought sourly, to wave goodbye to her gruff ex-smotherer and philanthropic paramour. But now she lingered a moment longer, fingers lightly gripping the BRC at breast-height; and I saw that she was looking at the vagrant . . . looking at him with a sort of tutelary patience . . . and that the vagrant was looking back at her, with an expression I couldn't quite name.

I glanced from one to the other—from bare feet to bare feet, from matted locks to ex-curlered, untidy curls—and realized, startled, that, across the width of that quiet Woodbrook street, dishevelment was considering dishevelment.

Then the woman locked the gate and went in, picking up the plastic thing from the sill in passing, closing the glass-paned door behind her. And the vagrant turned and walked away without a parting glance at me, walking now not with a vagrant's swagger but as any man would walk, going unhurriedly about his business, on a normal weekday morning—and *that*, I suddenly understood, had been the expression on the vagrant's face which I'd be unable to name.

From behind her garden gate, she had turned to him her unmade-up, naked-sad face: looking at him not as one man's housewife, nor another man's whore, but as a woman: just a woman. And from the pitiless glare of a shadeless pavement, he, the vagrant, had looked back at her, not with the bright eyes of his kind, nor with anything even remotely resembling a lecher's leer, but levelly, steadily, as a man considers a woman who means something to him. As a man. Just a man.

They were sobering, somehow wondrous, realizations. And, left alone on that empty Woodbrook street with the occasional car coming down it, I stood there for a long time, in my shrinking pool of shade (until, as he'd promised, my Good Samaritan returned in the white Galante, with his "electrics guy"), musing over all that I had seen.

PART IV

LOSING CONTROL

SONGSTER

BY JENNIFER RAHIM

North Coast

(Originally published in 2002)

Miss Ivy say she hear a singing trail through the church, sounding just like when Michael use to raise a few songs after the fishing done, and he by himself in *Queen Penny* bailing water in the shallows. His voice walking easy over the water and up the beach to where Mr. Oswald, who own the boat, and Sunil, the other fella that fish with them, checking the lines to see that everything ready for the next trip.

Everybody in Victory Bay know that Michael could sing. The boy have voice oiled and smooth like the Birdie crooning only a fool breaks his own heart. That is how he get the name Songster. So when Miss Ivy swear is Michael spirit that pass through the gathering last Good Friday, during the time that Pastor Williams call the church to silence so memory could swell and speak love for the dead, people didn't object, and some, like Mother Francis and Mr. David even, nod their heads as a confirmation. Is true, Michael not resting.

Nobody jump just so and believe any word Miss Ivy bring and that is because when she make baptism and Pastor Williams and the appointed believers lay hands and pray down the Spirit, Miss Ivy like she decide, when she raise up from where she get slain, that she is chief anointed prophet and seer of the Calvary Hill Renewal Temple of the Word. She say she see heaven open up like how it open for St. Stephen, and a man in white robes stretch out a long golden rod and touch her tongue.

Since then every time you look sharp is like prophecy dropping from the sky freesheet, and bad spirit following everybody. Then Pastor, who don't like to cross a soul and believe that everybody have to make their journey, decide to put his foot down when the prophecy come from Miss Ivy that the doc himself send a message that the country in a royal mess since he gone, and because he can't leave his people in need, he want everybody to pray to him for the party to rise again like in '56. Well, that is when Pastor put a ban on Miss Ivy prophesying.

Michael coulda sing anything, just call the tune and he gone clear with the lyrics, just like how kingfisher get carried away with their song when morning come, sweet too bad, and even the bed-sick get up and walk. So when Miss Ivy say his spirit still walking and that he singing, the church wasn't too quick to dismiss her word. Michael was a man who, when the mood take him, use to turn up in the middle of the service on a Sunday morning. He sit down quiet-quiet in the back listening to the lesson, not even joining in the amen-chorus when Pastor speak a truth that call for confirmation. Michael just sit there listening, with his eyes close, like he praying, although he is a man who make it clear to everybody that life have to live and you can't hide in no church. And is so Naomi plead with him not to talk so. That God don't sleep and that a man is more than the bread he labour for.

But everybody know Michael heart is gold and that is why he couldn't resist the church even though he stay by himself in the back. So he stay until Mother Crichlow raise a hymn he know, like "The Lord Is My Shepherd," that she bring out in a kind of long elastic wail, sounding like pain and victory, conviction and plea, all mix up in one. That is when out of nowhere Michael voice come sailing in, not drowning out nobody, but easing a kind of lightness and sweetness into the mournful stream of the congregation singing as if the hymn is a testimony to a faith they had to carry like a cross through their days. Singing a hope that heavy with the weight of a belief they had to pick up every day and roll away from their living, when poor people have children to feed, work to find, sick that can't pay for doctor, sons lost to rum and white powder, daughters with belly and no man to take responsibility, house to finish build, and nowhere to turn, and a life that asking every morning for a chance to live, demanding a chance to feel that this Victory Bay that have the taste and smell of salt is a home in truth.

In the middle of that kind of tormented faith, Michael singing break in from the back bench where he sitting by himself, with only old man Toby on the other end, close to the door, only because the bad chest-cold he get so long ago wouldn't leave him. Michael voice like a firm but sweet seconds-pan teasing out a rhythm that make the tired hymn sound new, pulling the voices together, and carrying their loads with its spirit that fresh like river water and the strong purpose of trees, reminding the church just where it going and what it dreaming. And Naomi so proud, she just sit down on the front bench rocking and softly praying, "Merciful Lord, mercy," with a kind of gratitude that everybody feeling, and they glad to hear somebody testifying to how their hearts find wings again in the beauty of Michael's voice.

That his spirit not at rest didn't come as no surprise. Everybody know Michael never do bad to nobody. In fact, from the day he born, Naomi swear he was a godsend, an angel that come to spend time with her. And everybody know that since he small Michael love to help people out. That is how he live, giving whatever he could give. Whatever you want—a hand to raise a roof, some small change to buy a little kerosene, a chicken coop to fix, fishing line to untangle, walls whitewash for Christmas—Michael there ready to help.

"What I go do now?" is what Naomi bawl when Esa pull her away from the body, and the truth finally sink in that he gone, and her wailing so loud it drown out the sound of the surf that racing up the beach and steady licking his bare feet like a dog trying to wake up his master. "Get up, Michael, get up, son!" And nobody could say a word. Not a sound from the crowd that gather on the beach to see the thing that shock the whole of Victory that Good Friday. Up to this day a heaviness resting on the village for the way Michael get gun down in broad daylight, and nobody could make sense of the madness that make the security pull the trigger.

Naomi wail come from way down in their own sorrow and anger and helplessness that is more than the vexation they feel for Hard Man who sit down in jail with no representation. Is the Syrians who come with they money and they big-shot connections that make them feel they have more rights than anybody so they could claim the beach and push the village out.

What they could say to Naomi? Everybody know Naomi was Michael queen. Mammy boy. Everything he do, he had his mother in mind. The same laths and the secondhand galvanize he buy two by two to fix up Naomi roof that falling down is what Guts and the boys use to raise a tent for the wake on Glorious Saturday, a day when people should be getting ready to sing Alleluia on Easter Sunday morning.

"Why they kill meh one good son?" Naomi ask and ask.

And the church, gathered to remember Michael, stand witness again to her relived sorrow. And as if she know that the silence that follow was too heavy for people to carry, that they need to remember again the rightness of their still-raw grief, Miss Ivy start to preach.

"Michael not resting. Oh no!" she say. "You know why? Is because of the injustice, the boldface-ness, the underhand dirtiness of them people who bring nothing but trouble to Victory because they feel they could own even God sea. And that Hard Man. Well, Lord have mercy on black people 'cause that boy is one of we, and is the white people money, the might he feel guarding they property that foolish Hard Man head and make him forget that he is a human being like everybody else. That is what went straight to his head and make him turn gun on Michael. Money, brethren, is what make some people feel they have more rights than everybody else. I telling you that is the disease that Hard Man catch. But God don't sleep."

She move from the benches to stand up in front of the church where all eyes could see her, and Pastor Williams, realizing that she riding with the Spirit, step aside to let her have her say.

"Greed!" she shout, pushing her bulk up on her toes as though she trying to gain height to seal her conviction. "The greed of people that can't satisfy till they buy heaven self, I not 'fraid to talk it, brothers and sisters. But we know them people." And she thrust out her hand in the direction of the resort, holding it stiff and deliberate like the rod of correction self. "They up to no good and that is what send Michael to his grave, big Good Friday when people should be praying, studying how them hard-hearted Pharisee hang Jesus up on a cross because he show them up, expose they wickedness, and all he wanted to do was love people."

And the church chorus, "Amen, sister! Speak it."

"That boy only do good for people. Yes, is somebody have to give due account for the innocent blood that shed. Yes, Father, on Good Friday self one year to this very day and justice not served!"

"Not served!" the church answer.

Is so Miss Ivy put it and nobody disagree with her words. Then, as if her testimony give little Laura courage to speak her heart, she bring her word even though is not a good year since she baptize. Laura, holding onto Papa Joseph hand, begin to tell how Michael spirit was really there in the service that morning, because when the church was quiet with only the low moaning and rocking because everybody praying deep, the same time that Miss Ivy say she hear him singing, that was when a cool-cool breeze stop just so and sweep through the gathering where everybody pack up tight like sardine in ten o'clock hot sun, and she feel her Uncle Michael passing. She say he smell like when he bathe off and dress up for Sunday evening and douse-down in Papa Joseph Old Spice cologne that he get every Christmas without fail from his daughter. Naomi always making joke that Mama Louise like her men smelling sweet, so she plan to keep up the tradition now that Mama dead and gone.

And that was when Naomi really start to cry.

"Out of the mouth of babes shall spring forth the truth!" Pastor proclaim.

And the church say, "Amen!"

Poor little Laura heart nearly break believing that she do some unspeakable crime and she run quick to hug up Naomi, saying over and over again, "Sorry, Grannie, sorry."

Papa Joseph had to take the child in the back of the church and try to soothe her. "Hush, dou-dou," he say in his gentle way, and his voice ringing with a kind of pride. That was how the congregation get to know that the child have the gift to see spirits. So while they feeling how Naomi pain open up like a wound, they glowing inside to see how the church get bless and knowing that Susan, who all the way up in New York working hard like a dog, would be proud to hear how Laura growing up close to the Lord.

Naomi cry so hard for her son that is like three o'clock Good Friday afternoon come back again and Sunil running up from the beach shouting, "Oh God, they shoot Michael!" At first people only stare like they didn't want to believe, but everybody hear the gunshot that blast away the usual deadness of the hour when not even dog have courage to bark. Then is like feet decide before head that Sunil wasn't tripping because next thing the whole of Victory Bay fly down to see where Michael lie down with a hole in his chest and his two eye open like he don't believe that is dead he dead.

Is so Naomi cry again, raw like on that same day when Esa had to hold her back from the body because she pick up the boy by his shoulders and start to shake him, bawling, "Wake up, son! Wake up! Somebody wake him up!" And the crowd stand up like they don't know what to do, like they 'fraid to meet the naked plea in her eyes, since what she asking make them feel their own smallness that they can't do nothing to help. They can't fight death. Is Esa who had to break through the circle and lead Naomi away slow-slow. She hold Naomi head on her shoulder all the way and Naomi saying over and over again, "He only just leave home to breeze out little bit on the beach." And Esa crooning to her like she is a child, saying, "Is okay, mother, hush-hush now," and all the while her own face wash with tears that she didn't have time to heed.

Hard Man, the security, stand behind the chain-link fence

in his black overalls and sunglasses, staring out at the crowd like what he seeing have nothing to do with him, even though he still holding the gun that hang down in his hand as if he don't even know it there. He just stare and his mouth half open behind the fence, and the two big guard dogs barking and running wild-wild up and down like they gone crazy. Nobody see the Syrian and them who own the place. They never come out. They never come to the wake or the funeral. They didn't even send flowers. People say they wasn't there that day. But later somebody report that they see a face by the window upstairs, a face that nobody could name, only that it was there, witness to the whole thing.

The church see it again, just like Naomi say. Michael watching the road from the gallery while Guts busy quarrelling about the Syrian people who move in on Victory Bay about two years ago and start one time to build fence right across the track that leading down to the beach where fishermen anchoring boats longer than anybody could remember. "You know what that man watch me in my face and say, Songster, when I tell the stone-faced Syrian that it don't have no other way to get down to the beach? Boy, that man, with his breath full up of whiskey and the gold chain shining in the sun with crucifix resting on he chest, watch me, as man, and say the track cutting through his property so the fishermen have to either anchor somewhere else or go all the way around Salvation headland. Go 'round Salvation my ass!"

"Take it easy on the language, man," Michael warn, but in a kind of voice that tell Guts he with him. It was just that he want Guts to remember he was in his mother yard and she don't stand for that type of talk, especially on Good Friday.

Michael listening but his mind was travelling, a thing that happen with him every now and again, so much so that Papa

Joseph, who outlive his own son as he like to boast, warn him already not to study life too deep. "Boy, you will tire your soul. One day at a time, man, one day at a time."

Maybe it was good advice, but Michael use to wonder if he do like Papa Joseph say, he use to wonder what he will miss out on becoming, what he will regret that he didn't build. "But a man have to plan his life, not so?" he ask Papa Joseph. And Papa just laugh like he familiar with the idea, but that it was the kind of thing not to take serious because it prove wrong long time. Is just that Michael too young to know. Or maybe he laugh because the idea remind him of something he wanted to forget. Maybe he didn't have the courage to remember what he never do as a man, so he laugh to throw a blanket over the emptiness inside that he didn't fill, or couldn't fill. He laugh because it so true what Michael say that the pain the truth cut in him make him want to ease the hurt little bit.

But Michael never really know what was behind Papa Joseph mantra, *One day at a time, man*. What he sure about, as he tell anybody who willing to listen, is that life can't live just so. You have to decide how you want to shape it, like how the children take the sand on the beach and build all kind of fancy house and thing, the same sand that everybody walking on, he watch how they dream it into shapes. "That is how you have to live."

So it was not that he didn't care about what Guts was saying. In fact, everything Guts talk about was why his mind was travelling. Michael think hard about the Syrian and them who come to set up some kind of private club for people from Port of Spain to have a good time and bathe in clean north coast water, soak up sun and drink whiskey all weekend. He think about Hard Man and how he walking up and down the Syrian yard with walkie-talkie in his hand, beeper on his hip, and talk say he even have gun for guarding the white people property. And in between sucking toothpick all day, he chatting up the girls from the composite school, showing off with his walkie-talkie and passing five dollar to the ones who bold enough to answer his challenge to take.

Just so Hard Man move from hustling ten days all over the place, as far as Grande, to watchman work on the Syrian property. And people feel it have more in the mortar because things look like it going real nice with him. Hard Man neck shining with gold and when he turn up by the snackette to shoot pool with the fellas on his day off, is brand-new threads he sporting and Johnnie Walker he drinking, straight up. Everybody suspicious about what really happening in the place but nobody have anything concrete to move on. All they could get out of Hard Man is his anthem, "Them Syrian have money to throw way, partner!" and he do a kind of one-two move, sliding his waist dainty-dainty and holding up his hands like he dancing a set with somebody, just like the white fella who break ranks and singing calypso in tents all over Port of Spain, sink or float.

But Michael was also thinking about Esa, who come with the news that Hard Man make a move on her the other evening when she was passing through the track as usual to meet him down by the boat. She say how he appear out of nowhere and stop her just so. "You trespassing, lady. You have to pay to pass," Esa say he tell her, and his hand reach and grab hold of his crotch and he start to smile like he already doing to her what he thinking.

"I will kill him if he touch you. Let him touch you!" His anger had scared them both and she throw her arms around his neck and hold him to calm him because she didn't want nothing to happen now that the baby coming.

"Baby?" he say and pull away to watch her straight in her face. She wasn't going to tell him then, but something in his anger, in the pure strength and purpose of it, reach right into where the child was resting and tell her the time was right to open her secret.

"Baby?" That was what make the ground he was standing on shift and then he had to reach out and hold her to steady himself. He hold on as though he finally find the anchor he was looking for, and after the truth finish rock him, he said it: "We getting married." Straight so. He didn't have to think and he know it was because the decision was only waiting for him all this time to claim it. "After the child born, we going to do it." And this time he hug her with the yes of his embrace that was also his decision to put things in place—money for the wedding and to fix up a place for Esa and the baby.

She simply look at him and answer, "Yes," as if a world open up that was bigger than the two of them. And that was what really settle it for him, the yes that sound like a surrender to a future.

Then there was *Queen Penny* rocking peaceful down in the bay. She had some years on her but she was a good, sturdy craft. That was his future, and Esa's. Two more payments and Mr. Oswald would hand her over. That was their agreement when he tell Michael he was giving up the fishing to go States-side by his daughter.

"I getting old," he say. "Forty-five years I in this," and he look out across the wide blue of the bay.

A kind of sadness come down between them that make Michael joke, "But you have plenty in you still, man. What you mean you getting old?"

It was late and nobody was on the beach then, only the anchored boats bucking on the waves and two strays combing the water's edge for fish guts. Mr. Oswald give a little laugh just to show he know the game and pass his hand down the front of his bare chest that still show his power, although the skin no longer smooth and tight. Tide was in and the bay look full and settle. Mr. Oswald take a deep breath like a man who trying to touch once again what he know to be true about himself.

"The sea is a good life for fellas with the belly. Peter not interested. He set on wearing police uniform. Pretty-boy work, but that is his choice. I not meddling. So is only me now with Maureen done married and settle down up in Florida. She say she want me to come up and take things easy for a change. Take things easy."

Michael listen to him repeat the line and he wonder if Mr. Oswald was trying to teach himself what they might mean. He was a man seasoned on hard work, getting up four o'clock every morning so that before five he guiding *Queen Penny* out the bay, and he know he not setting foot on land until next day same time. Sun and rain beating down on his back while he waiting for what the sea will give him. Michael watch him walk to where the surf hustling up the beach. He walk into the water a little way then, bend down and draw up a handful to wash his face.

"The boat is yours if you want it," he say without turning around to face him. "We could work something out with the payments. But I giving you first choice." With that he start to wade slowly toward the deep and then he disappear beneath the swelling surf.

Not even his mother know what Michael and Mr. Oswald plan. Michael wanted it to be a surprise when he stand up on the day the last payment make and tell her that he own a boat. That was what he wanted. To announce his ownership—not that he feel it would make him a man or make people see him. No, the boat was a signal to himself and to everybody of his decision to claim his space in the world and to make his future real. Two more payments. That was all.

But now the Syrians come and make life hard for everybody by trying to control access to the beach.

"They wrong," Guts was still complaining. "That is a public beach and everybody damn well know that you can't pass Salvation side even in low tide, and besides, who he think he is to tell me where to anchor my boat? That out there is God sea, man."

After that Guts get silent as if he tired, too tired to even quarrel again. He sit down on the step with one leg cross tight over the other. Is all his life, since he old enough to handle his own line, Guts fishing in north coast waters with his father, and anchoring *Saga Boy*, the boat that he take over when old man St. Clair pass on. It use to be *Promise Land* then, but Guts say with his father dead and gone a new time start. So the same week that St. Clair bury, Guts decide to rename the boat. He get Miss Ivy son, Santo, who could paint sign good though is mostly road work he doing, to write *Saga Boy* on the bow in red, yellow, and green, with fancy lettering that look like waves. That is how he tell Santo to make them: "Like waves cruising in on the bay."

But that was not enough, because like Guts wanted to make a big statement about his life now that he was in charge of his own boat. Like he wanted to say to the people that he not no little boy, although nobody would look at Guts with his salt-and-pepper head of hair and think he was no boy. It was like Guts wanted to announce his independence and to tell the world that he was the owner now that his father gone. So he buy two bottle of rum and some beer from by Harry, a fella from Grande who come all the way to Victory Bay to set up a "modern establishment," as he like to call it.

Harry Recreational Club and Bar was the full name, the first of its kind on the coast that have pool table and a second-hand arcade game called Speedway that always have about three or so young fellas glue onto the screen any time of the day, "wasting they mother money," according to Naomi. Santo self paint the sign that cause big quarrel between him and Harry when some white man who on holiday sightseeing stop and say is bad English Santo paint. In the end they decide to leave the sign rather than squeeze in the apostrophe, which would only cause it to look choke up.

So Guts boat get baptize, with some fellas on the beach drinking rum and beer from Harry club, talking and cussing politicians until it get dark and the bottles empty.

That was before the Syrians come and say the estate that stretching for seven acres on the coast side of the main road is their own. As long as anybody could remember, that same estate was only bush with one or two mango tree and coconut growing on it. But the owners come to claim it and in two-twos a van with some men pull up. Then a truck come and drop material and fence start to go up, beginning from Salvation headland on the east where Prophet meditate every morning for twenty years before he pass away, and use to say he could hear Africa clear-clear from there. The fence stretch from Salvation right down to the boundary with the Breezy Ridge property that the retired English doctor own. No beach down below, only rocks and sea where they say the doc wife fall from trying to fly back home on whiskey and coconut water.

"Only four feet of land—that is all the Syrian have to give up to leave the track open for we to reach the beach," Guts say all of a sudden, breaking up the silence. "You think that is asking too much, Songster? Four feet of land . . . and now he want to build wall all the way down the slope to make sure we can't get through."

"Well, it look like them people don't want we on they beach. They don't want fish guts stinking up they place. Maybe it not about the land because between you and me, four feet a land ain't mean nothing to a man with seven whole acres in his hand. Maybe they trying to tell we that we not welcome to use the same sea with them and they Port of Spain friends. Maybe they don't want we close enough to interfere with they business, get in the way of they privacy. Is really about us, Guts, not the land. Is we they fighting to fence out."

"Fence we out! Man, I born in this village. My father and grandfather dead right here. I go dead here too. Fence me out because I on . . . that is God sea, man. You ain't hear me. That is God sea!"

Guts small frame get rigid and Michael hold the challenge in his hard stare long enough for him to recognize that he too carrying the same pain. And it was only then that the anger subside in him and his body relax and there was nothing more to say.

Guts pick up and say he gone to cool-out by the school-ground where bachelors batting against married men. Michael watch him until he disappear down the road. Then his mind stay with *Queen Penny*. He study how she must be just rolling lazy from side to side in the bay. Wednesday morning was the last time she went out with only he and Mr. Oswald. Sunil didn't go that time. He miss again because he was sick, or that is what his mother send Kamal to say.

"He sick bad. Doh want to eat self." His eyes remain plant on the ground like he shame or 'fraid. Michael only listen but all the time feeling like he want to tell the boy that he don't have nothing to 'fraid, that he could look up off the ground and see that the world not judging him, not him. But he didn't say nothing because he didn't want to make it any harder for the boy. He didn't want him to know that he hear the whole story already. So he just let Kamal finish the message that he memorize.

The little fella look so shame. That is what really hurt Michael, that the boy carrying all that weight for nothing. The jersey Kamal wearing hang up on him and it have a dirty print of the Statue of Liberty that mark *I Love New York*. Kamal finger hook up in a hole in front. The finger twirl and twirl, stretching out the hole while he talking. And Michael heart all the time feeling like it want to break. He want to run over by Sunil and shake him for not staying away from the poison Lion pushing. Sunil anthem fix in his head like a beat-up ballad.

"I done with smoking, Songster. I done. Lion could keep he powder." He swallow down the beer Michael just buy for him, his hand shaking as he try to steady the empty bottle on the counter. "I could stop any time I want, and this time, man, I not getting tie up in that thing again. Look how thin I getting."

Michael avoid looking at him as if he didn't need the confirmation or he couldn't bear to fix his eyes on the truth that raw as flesh on Sunil lips, a truth that he choose to hide from his own self like a man trying to hide from his shadow.

That was the same day Hard Man crawl into the bar, prop the sunglasses up on his head and order a bottle of rum loud for everybody to hear. Then deliberate like he turn to face Michael and Guts, "You fellas drinking?" and before they could answer, he tell Harry wife who was working that day to bring two clean glass for his pardners. "Help yehself," he say.

Sunil ain't wait a second before he start to pour a straight rum for himself, while Michael sit down there watching Hard Man in his face.

"What happen, man, you not drinking my rum?" and he start to laugh so mucus that everybody turn around to see what was happening.

"I doh drink bad rum," Michael answer and he ask Harry wife to bring another beer for him. "Real cold," he say and he keep his eyes hook on Hard Man. The place get dead with only the music blasting in vain from the speakers. Everybody watching to see what going to happen.

Hard Man pretend he get cuff in his face and he stagger back a few steps. "Oui, boy, you hitting hard today! But suit yourself."

But the whole thing so false that nobody even laugh and Hard Man look around as if he want to make sure that the bar was his audience. Then he take up the bottle and walk toward the section with the pool table, moving like a man who know he on show and that he sure the danger he feeling in his own blood expose. Just when Hard Man certain he in full view of all who in the place, he stop and take a hit straight from the bottle like he is a badjohn in a old western.

"You doh have to drink my rum, Songster. No sir, but I go drink what is yours any day. That is a nice woman you have there, man. A nice woman." He never turn to face Michael, not because he 'fraid. No, he wanted to give him his back before he raise up his hands above his head, one holding the rum bottle, and start to do a wicked wine to the chutney tune that was blasting from Harry speaker boxes.

"Whey! That is wine, brother!" somebody bawl out from the shadows of the bar.

The beer bottle just miss his head and explode on the far

wall. Hard Man freeze. The place get like a cemetery when like in slow motion he turn around this time to face Michael, his right hand prop in front by his waist balancing on something below his shirt.

"Is me you want to hit, man? Is me?" he say, making as though he could hardly believe Michael try to lick him down.

Then the shout ring out, "He have a gun, Songster!"

Same time Harry dash out from somewhere behind the counter and start to hustle Michael toward the road. "No fighting in here, man. Not in here." And Sunil too was pushing him from behind, "Cool it, man. Let we go from here. Forget he, man. Let we go."

"She sweet too bad!" Hard Man shout behind them. And when Michael, who was in a tight vise between Harry and Guts, get a chance to glance back, Hard Man was dancing out in front of the shop with Pearlie, one of the regulars, a signal to the entire village that he claim victory, and sealing at the same time his right to do what he want. And Sunil only repeating, "Leave him, Songster, leave the man alone."

So when Kamal finish giving his message, Michael just dip in his pants pocket and fish out the last three dollars he find, put it in the boy hand and say, "Give that to your mother."

Not even then the boy lift his eyes to meet his. He just speed out of the yard like he running away from the shame and the gratitude that get mix up in his abrupt, "Thanks, Mr. Michael."

All that—the Syrians, Esa, *Queen Penny*, Sunil, everything Guts say—roll up in one hard ball and stink in his chest so Michael feel he need to breathe again. That is when he decide to take a turn down by the beach.

"I tell him don't go in the sea," Naomi announce to the church. "I tell him people not to bathe in the sea on Good Friday. And he tell me he just going to breeze out little bit. That is all. He say he not bathing."

Naomi pause and the silence so heavy it get hard to even breathe. "Right there they shoot my boy, right on his spot. He never go close to the white people place. Is right there they shoot the boy where he use to tease me and say he could look out at the horizon and see the future. Right there . . . that was all he went down on the beach for, to sit down on his spot and dream about where he was going."

And that was when Esa come forward from where she was sitting down next to Mother Crichlow, who is the great-aunt that grow her. Esa hand Miss Ivy the baby and straightaway throw her arms around Naomi and start to rock. "Michael gone, Mama Naomi, he gone. Let him go," she say. "We have to let him go." And so she rock Naomi until she get quiet again. Then Mother Crichlow raise a hymn and the church start to sing, *Then sings my soul, my saviour God to Thee. How great Thou art! How great Thou art!*" And Pastor step up to Naomi and lay hands on her head and start to pray loud for healing, and for Michael spirit to leave the living and find peace. And all the while the church sing strong and steady like is Jesus self they want to make come down from the cross and ease the pain and the hope that tighten in everybody throat.

The singing build and build till it swell like a wave threatening the shore, and just as it get to a point where the emotion ready to break loose, Sister Elsie ring the brass bell one, two, three times and is heaven self open and rain down mercy because everything that they carrying, all that they feeling, come rushing out. All Naomi loss and pain, their own grief and anger, because Michael gone too soon.

Who will believe Sunil, the only man that see how Hard

Man pull the trigger when Michael stand up with nothing but words for his weapon? These days Sunil dragging himself all over the place like he don't have no home, no name. And is true Hard Man sit down in jail, but he have his own story about self-defense because Michael had a score to settle and all he do was try to protect himself. Against what? A man with empty hands? Against words? As if words could break bones. Chut, man! And the Syrians still there, fencing up the place. They go on like nothing happen, fête throwing almost every weekend as normal, and they have a new security in black overalls with walkie-talkie and sunglasses, walking up and down the yard. The fellas on the block call him Carbon Copy.

All that and more pour out and the singing start to subside again, not because is defeat they accept, but because in the singing they hear again their promise and strength to suffer the right to be there in Victory Bay like they was people in truth with flesh that could feel and love and dream. They sing until they convince themselves again that they real and their living was an acceptance that not even death, or the Syrian who own the politicians and the lawyers, could deny them. It was only then that the singing ease into a stillness that hold everybody like an answer that asking its own question about their acceptance.

Is like the silence wake up Esa baby because all the time, through all the service, he sleeping a sweet sleep and just so he open up his lungs and announce his presence. "But look at my crosses," Miss Ivy say, "this child practicing scales."

And everybody laugh and agree how the boy following his father. That was what make Naomi rise up from her grief and tell Esa to bring the child and she hold him up right there in the front bench like she seeing him for the first time. Then she tell Esa, "Is time we christen this child. We wait too long to name the boy and present him to the Lord. Esa, what you calling this boy child?"

And Esa swallow hard and her two eye full up as she watch the boy how he smiling back at Naomi face and say, "Michael. I calling him Michael."

That Easter Sunday Naomi cook a big feast. "Is a feast for Michael," she say, "and I want everybody to come." That was all and nobody dare to ask for more. So after the service, with the *Alleluia* still singing in their blood, the whole church end up by Naomi house. Everybody was there, down to Sunil who try to stay clean for the day though he look all the time like he want to run away. Naomi fry chicken and curry duck. Sunil mother help Esa make the dhalphouri, and they work so nice together Naomi make a joke and say they better open a roti shop in front the house. It even had Mother Crichlow special pepper sauce and Guts get the fishermen to chip up and they buy white rum with Harry throwing in a free bottle as his contribution. On top of that Naomi bring out the cashew wine she curing for two whole years.

People eat and drink and fête to Papa Joseph cuatro till Monday come. And just before midnight when Guts head was hot with rum and talk about the fisherman union that he calling the fellas to start to put pressure on the Syrians and to guard their affairs, Naomi take baby Michael in her arms and walk out to the road with him. She could see the Syrian place, how it light up with all the doors and windows wide open, and people was fêteing on the verandah to a tune the Birdie sing about a man in the queen bedroom. But Naomi ain't take them on. From the house it look like she was showing Michael the stars.

THE PARTY

by Elizabeth Walcott-Hackshaw
Santa Cruz Valley
(Originally published in 2007)

> *I'll love you, dear, I'll love you*
> *Till China and Africa meet,*
> *And the river jumps over the mountain*
> *And the salmon sing in the street.*
> —W.H. Auden

Tricia shook her head and smiled, she was frying the polori balls for the party as she told Miss Alice the story of the piper-pimp and his two lady friends who had cleaned out Miss John's house while she was away, visiting her daughter "in foreign." They stole everything: fridge, stove, fans, dishes, glasses, pots, clothes, sheets, even Miss John's bras; the only things they left behind were her Bible, hymn book, and two lightbulbs. Everyone on Blackman Street heard the deep howl as the poor old lady walked into her house the night she returned from Brooklyn.

"Imagine those people buy them things knowing that it belong to their own neighbour. The piper and his lady friends have so much crack in their head 'fus they stupid enough to sell the things on the same street where they thief it." Tricia laughed her high-pitched laugh, shook her head again, then took out another batch of golden polori balls and placed them on a sheet of neatly spread white napkins to absorb all the excess oil. The kitchen was filled with the delicious smell of geera and masala, frying in garlic, onions, and yellow curry powder.

Alice smiled as she arranged the samosas and mini rotis she had ordered onto a large white platter. She loved to hear Tricia's stories; they had spent a lot of time this way, Tricia cooking and Alice listening to Tricia's stories about the village.

"When they catch them I hear they put plenty licks on them in the station. Sergeant Socks doh make joke, he doh stand for any stupidness, a real church man, every Sunday up in front, right next to Miss John and Father." Tricia claimed that the piper confessed in less than half an hour and minutes later the police went into all the houses on the street to search for the stolen items.

"You should see the neighbours, they so shame to show how much they buy from the piper. Ma John get everything back except the fridge, for some reason they can't find the fridge. No matter how much licks they put on the piper he doh want to tell Sergeant Socks who have the fridge. Five years they give him, yes, and they say Socks tell him to go and chill out in prison and see how many fridges he go steal there."

Both Alice and Tricia giggled together. Alice felt lucky to have Tricia around, she could always tell a good story and make Alice laugh. Tricia lived on the same street as poor Miss John, Blackman Street, in an area they called "the village," five minutes by car from Alice's home, which the people from Tricia's village called "the vale." Every area in Pastora Valley had a name.

From the kitchen window Alice could see that the ashes were still falling even though the fires had stopped earlier that morning. They weren't the thick black ones that fell while the hills were still ablaze, but the thin ones, like strips of grey paper, light and weightless. Ashes had been falling in Pastora Valley for months, ever since the dry-season fires had begun in January. Sometimes they fell at night, or late evening, or even during the morning when the sun blazed through the valley like a torch. But the ashes seldom fell at two o'clock in the afternoon. That year every field in the valley, all the hills, the cocoa estates, and the pawpaw fields were dry; the valley was like a desert, shades of brown were everywhere—the leaves were a nut brown, the grass a golden brown, the earth a brown brown and the hills more black than brown. All the lawns (except the ones in the vale where the owners used sprinklers illegally at night) had dried up. A thick layer of smoke often hovered over the valley during the day and sometimes veiled all of the hills.

Alice went onto the covered part of the kitchen veran-dah where she usually had the birthday parties for Emma. She had to wait to see when the ashes would stop falling before she laid everything out on the long teak table she had inher-ited from her mother; when she was a child her mother would dress the table, the same teak table, for the beautiful Christ-mas lunch. Alice loved the weather at Christmas, the strong winds, the cool air; she missed the Christmas weather and everything that reminded her of her mother. "Muggy" would be her mother's word for this weather, but for Alice it was just too hot, like some sort of hell.

Tricia covered all the bowls and platters with clear plastic wrap: the chocolate, coconut, and vanilla fudge, the pink-and-white sugar cakes, the pinwheel cheese-paste sandwiches, the sausage rolls, the meat pies, the corn curls, the tortilla chips, the potato chips, the cupcakes, and the huge bowl of lollipops. Tricia would wait before she put everything out, wait for the ashes to stop falling. Then Alice would dress the table with the allamanda and the fuchsia bougainvillea that grew along the edge of the front porch.

In the early mornings, before this terrible dry season, before Alice began her morning routine of filling Emma's lunch-kit or making breakfast for Emma and Scott, she would open the door and step onto the kitchen verandah; she loved the hills at the back of the house and the feel of that cool morning air on her face, the mist lifting like a curtain to reveal waves of sea-green hills. But these days, with all the fires, the early-morning air felt as though the valley had put on a thick woolen winter coat, so Alice stopped going outside. Except for this morning, for the first time in months, mainly because she couldn't sleep, and mainly because it was Emma's birthday she opened her doors to the hills in the valley but was disappointed at the sight of falling ashes.

Two nights before, Emma had run into Scott and Alice's bedroom with the deep scream children have when the fear sounds like a sharp pain. In between breaths, she told them she had heard seven gunshots in the hills (she had counted them), and she was sure that seven bandits were coming for her. Alice and Scott were already awake, they had heard the shots as well, there had been many more than seven; but to comfort Emma they lied and said that the boys in the village were just "bursting bamboo." They let Emma get into bed and lie between them.

During the long night Scott tried to calm Emma as more sounds of shots entered the bedroom. Their sleep was broken at best; Scott got up a few times to check on the dogs; the older two, terrified of the noise, were huddled near the tool-shed. In the morning Scott went to the police station to talk to Sergeant Socks. Since the dry season had begun Socks had stepped up the marijuana raids in the hills; he had already been featured twice on the evening news, standing in a field of marijuana holding his automatic weapon with heaps of ganja smoking in the background. Socks told Scott that a raid had taken place the night before to "smoke out" two bandits who were hiding in the hills. Socks loved to use American phrases like "smoke out," phrases he had heard on CNN. Before Scott left the Pastora station, Sergeant Socks reassured him there was nothing to worry about and Scott reminded him about Emma's birthday party. An invitation Socks had always received ever since Alice and Scott moved into Pastora Valley seven years ago.

At 2:15 p.m. Alice was just about to call the security company when she saw the van pull up to the gate. The two guards came up to the camera perched high above the left stone pillar; they pressed the buzzer and spoke through the intercom. Looking into the small TV screen in the kitchen, Alice recognized the twins who provided the security for the dinner party they had had a month ago for Scott's parents' fortieth anniversary. This was a party she felt forced to have; she had never gotten along with Scott's mother, and with things so tense between Scott and herself, the entire evening felt like hard work, with her acting the part of the contented wife and mother and smiling tight, wide smiles as the guests of honour were toasted again and again for forty more. That night Alice missed her mother more than ever; three years had already passed since she had lost her but the pain was still there, it was a nagging pain, numbed on busy days, paralyzing on others, so Alice felt as though it would never go away and in a strange way she didn't want it to. With all of Scott's family at the anniversary party she felt lonelier than ever.

The owner of the security company, Scott's second cousin

Jeffrey, was also invited to Emma's birthday party; his daughter Charlotte and Emma were the same age and in the same class at school. Alice opened the electric gates and the gleaming white pickup with the dogs caged in the van's tray drove up the winding gravel path and parked at the side of the house. The dogs were trying to poke their muzzled snouts through the spaces in the wire cage. Luckily Scott had already put their four rottweilers into the kennel. Only Netty, a skinny black mongrel, was still unleashed; she was a stray Alice had found two years ago at their beach house in La Fillette. Netty was friendly, harmless, protective, and at times quite fierce, as though forever grateful for Alice's good deed. As soon as Scott saw the van he put down the weedwacker and went towards the security guards. His T-shirt was soaking with sweat; he had spent most of the morning with their gardener, Ricky, cutting down the dry bush around the edges of the property.

Alice was staring at Scott; just looking at him made her angry. He could be smiling, walking, drinking a cup of coffee, playing with Emma or the dogs, and she would feel like slapping and scraping him over and over again. They had been having the same fight for the last two years; things would calm down for a month or so, sometimes more, and then something would trigger it to start all over again. The months of counselling, the vacations to the Bahamas, London, and Paris, the separation, the short-lived reconciliation, the brief honeymoons— none of it could get rid of the intense desire she had on some days to hurt him badly, the way he had hurt her when she found out about his screwing that bitch Nalini. How many times had she warned Scott about Nalini? About what her friends called the Caroni Complex? Nalini was exactly one of those country Indians who had left the cane fields to find a sugar daddy in town. Her overfriendly manner, her willingness to work overtime, even on Sundays, her tacky, skanky outfits. But Scott never listened to Alice, or at least preferred not to.

"Eric. William. How's it going?" Scott shook their hands. Scott was always very good with names and with people; his job as director of the sales department in his father's marine equipment company demanded it.

"Afternoon, Mr. Charles," they both said in unison, in the same polite tone. "Sorry to be late, we had to wait for the dogs," Eric continued.

"No problem." Scott walked towards the kennel; the dogs were now going crazy, snarling and barking at each other. "Take your set around to the back to calm these down a little; we have a horse coming too." Scott didn't see the need to have horse rides, a bouncy castle, and two children's makeup artists all for a six-year-old's party, but he was still doing as much as he could to keep Alice calm, if not happy, today. He tried to convince himself that she had actually forgiven him for the night he had spent with his former secretary Nalini two years ago; that one-night stand, that one drunk, fucked-up fuck had cost him two years and counting. Scott tried to convince himself that things would get back on track, the way they were before Nalini. Early on, after he was cornered by Alice and like an idiot confessed, he felt like running away, taking Emma and moving out, because he couldn't stand the torture of the never-ending interrogations, the silences that could last for days, or the constant badgering, the crying, the screaming, that feeling of apprehension, of tension, from the moment he walked in the door each evening. One night when he decided he couldn't keep paying for his crime any longer, he drove off, leaving Alice screaming on the verandah, holding Emma. He stayed at his cousin Jeffrey's house for two days. Alice never called. But all Scott could think about was Alice and Emma and so he went back. Scott knew then that Alice would have to be the one to leave because he felt even more battered and broken away from her and from his Emma. They had known each other since high school, for goodness sake, but there were sides to Alice that Scott knew he would probably never understand. Beyond their own mess, she carried a sadness inside her, probably as a result of losing her father when she was only six, Emma's age. To survive, Scott tried hard not to think about what he had done or even Alice's unhappiness.

"Plenty bush fires up here, Mr. Charles?" Eric asked.

"Boy, endless, and the ashes only just settling down, earlier today they were falling like rain."

Eric and William both gave pleasant grunts, then worked quickly to get their two pit bulls out of the van's tray, away from Mr. Charles's dogs, and immediately began to patrol the perimeter of the backyard. They wore the usual uniform: black cargo pants tucked into black high-top boots, black short-sleeved shirts with two pockets on either side, guns in their holsters and wraparound black shades. They weren't the typical blue-black, stocky, muscular security guards that most companies used; Eric and William had light-brown skin, were slim and not very tall. They looked more like bank clerks, Alice thought, peering out at them from the kitchen window, but according to Jeffrey they were his best men.

The dogs finally settled down but all the noise had woken up Emma. Alice heard Emma's familiar scream for Tricia. They were all trying to let her nap as close to party time as possible. Although three thirty was the time on the invitations, Alice knew that most of the guests wouldn't arrive before four. Tricia had just stepped into the backyard to pick some dill and a little rosemary for the yogurt dip that Alice had taught her to make.

"Trish, Emma's up, I'll do the dip if you get her ready."

"Yes, Miss Alice." Tricia picked another sprig of rosemary and then hurried back inside. She washed her hands in the large kitchen sink, dried them with the towel on the counter, and left Alice opening the containers of plain yogurt for the dip.

Alice didn't look up at Tricia when she said, "The dress for the party is on the bed. Put her hair in a bun, she'll want to leave it out but it will get too messy. Thanks, Trish."

Tricia saw Eric and William walk by the perimeter of the porch; she knew them; they acknowledged her with a nod and moved the dogs away.

Tricia's only son, Tony, used to work for Mr. Jeffrey's security company as well, but the long hours, the good chance of being shot by some show-off bandit, and the minimum-wage paycheck made him leave. Things only got worse after he quit; he started liming with a group of young Muslimeen who claimed to be doing community work in the village; everyone knew they were selling drugs and looking for new recruits. Tricia and Tony fought daily about all the time he spent with them, until one day she came home from work to a neatly made bed and a note. It said that he believed that Islam was the path to his new God, Allah, and that she shouldn't worry because he would be taken care of by his Muslimeen brothers on their compound deep in the Sans Souci hills. Tricia could do nothing to get him back; her only consolation was that he wasn't in Sergeant Socks's area anymore; the last two Muslimeen youths from the village (boys no more than seventeen) were shot dead by Sergeant Socks right in front of Woo's Grocery. Socks and his men accused them of robbery and the attempted kidnapping of Mr. Woo himself. No one disagreed, not even Mr. Woo, even though everyone knew that Frank

Woo was burying his first cousin in Arouca that very Saturday. The rumour was that Socks shot those boys to send a message to their boss, the imam on the Sans Souci compound, who owed Socks a lot of money.

These days Tricia saw her son once a month. Tony, now Hassan Ali, would pull up to her gate in the village in his shiny black Sentra, never without two other "brothers" from his youth group; he'd blow the horn and she would come out. Tricia's neighbours in the village always paid attention when they saw the black car with the young Muslimeens driving up the street; if mothers were in their homes they peeped through their curtains and kept their young boys inside, but the young men liming on the corner hailed the car as it passed as though it were a chariot carrying kings. Later in the day, when Sergeant Socks came to make his rounds, they hailed his jeep in the same way.

Tony never got farther than the gate to mutter an "Assalam-u-alaikum," then a "Hello, Ma," handing her an envelope before he got back into the car with his brothers in their black shades, white robes, and white toupees. She took the money, never asking where it came from (things were just too hard now to think about that), half for her, half for Tony's child-mother and their baby girl, Fatima. In the early days after Tony left, Tricia would lie on her bed at night and weep, holding her belly like a child with a terrible stomachache, but now she just took the money and thanked God that her son was still alive. Tony, he was her only begotten son. She had had hopes for that boy; the teachers used to say how bright he was and she had worked hard to give him what she could, because for most of his life it had just been the two of them.

Upstairs Tricia had managed to get a still-drowsy Emma into the dress from her godparents, Jeffrey and his wife Kathy;

it was a deep pink, embroidered with small yellow-and-blue flowers around the sleeve, neckline, and hem. Emma's godparents had bought it on their last cruise to Mexico. Emma often resisted any suggestions Alice made about clothes, but she always accepted Tricia's without a fuss. So Alice usually had Tricia dress her for special occasions.

Alice put the dip in the fridge and went upstairs to Emma's room. From the doorway she saw Tricia combing Emma's thick, curly brown hair—hair Emma hated because it wasn't straight and smooth like Barbie's or silky and straight like her cousin Charlotte's. They were facing the window, not the door. Emma's room had one of the best views in the house; in the rainy season the two sets of large sliding windows opened up to the thick green valley hills, and in the dry season, if there weren't too many fires, the hills were orange and yellow from the immortelle and poui trees.

Alice looked at Tricia from the doorway. They were only a year apart, but Tricia was already a grandmother at forty. She had on an old floral dress Alice had given her a few years ago and a pair of Alice's old slippers. The angle of Tricia's body exposed a thin leg that looked dry, black, and powdery; the heel of her foot was flaking, the sole was thick and yellow; her body looked old but her voice was that of a young girl's. Alice often wondered what it would have been like if, in another life, things were turned around and she was the one working for Tricia in Tricia's old dress with her dry black skin, her kinky black hair, her two-room home, and this job, bringing up somebody else's child. When Emma was a baby, Tricia used to sing hymns to her from her church while she brushed her hair, but these last few months, ever since her son joined the Muslimeen, Alice noticed a change in Tricia. She still laughed when she told Alice stories about the village, but whenever

Tricia thought she was alone, Alice could see the sadness in her.

"You going to behave a nice girl at the party," Tricia said as she pulled Emma's hair into a perfect bun. Emma nodded.

"So tell Trish who coming to your party."

Emma began her list: "Charlotte, Juliette, Jean-Paul, Emily-Louise, Izzy, Tara . . ."

Alice walked away quietly, still hearing them chatting; she had hoped that the distance she felt between herself and Emma would get better with time, but it had only gotten worse, and what Scott had done didn't help. For some strange reason she had passed some of the anger she felt for Scott on to Emma. Or maybe she was always jealous of the way Scott treated Emma—he was so gentle with her, always trying his best not to hurt her. But it wasn't just Scott; Alice had always envied mothers, like her mother, like Tricia, who felt this closeness to their children right away and knew how to make it grow.

As Alice passed the large glass window along the corridor she noticed the twins, Eric and William, standing with their dogs like statues on either side of the entrance; by the time she got to her bedroom and looked again, they had disappeared.

Alice knew that this was not the best time to have a party. There had been so many kidnappings in the last few months that many of Emma's classmates had bodyguards as drivers. Only a year ago, if a parent couldn't make it, they would send the housekeeper or sitter; now they sent a bodyguard. Good security had to be provided at the parties, otherwise the parents would think twice about coming or sending their child. She didn't like having the parties, never had, even though she tried her best to hide that fact from both Scott and Emma with her wide smiles and supreme organization. She didn't like being inspected by the other mothers. In the beginning she tried to make an extra effort to keep up, spending the day at the salon, buying new outfits for herself, Emma, and even Scott. But lately what she wore to a birthday party seemed to matter less and less to her. Her standard khaki capri and a black T-shirt would have to do today.

When Scott and Alice first moved into Pastora seven years ago, having grown up in areas where grotesque sprawling houses covered most of the land, they were excited by all the green fields with the buffalypso, the old cocoa estates, and even the fires in the hills around the vale at night. Sometimes the valley would burn for days and nights, but after one heavy downpour of white rain it could renew itself again, with fresh razor grass reclaiming the burnt earth in what seemed like minutes. At night, during the dry season, they sometimes sat outside on the verandah to look at the fires; orange cinders sparkled against a pitch-black night with silvery blue stars and a thick, milky moon. The black hills resembled volcanoes, sending streams of lava into the valley below. Once, Alice even tried to write a poem about the valley at night using all the same words: *silvery blue stars, milky moon,* and *streams of lava,* but she never finished it.

Everyone said that this dry season was different not just in the valley but all over the island. There were fires everywhere on the hills, even along the highways, with flames sometimes licking the cars as they drove by. Hot, hazy mornings exposed the damage done the night before; the earth looked like chunks of coal and ashes, like there were mounds of salt everywhere. The local Venezuelan psychic said that the island was being punished for all the terrible crimes: "De kidnapping, de murder, de chile abuse, and de drogues, taking over." The leader of the largest Pentecostal church on the island, Pastor Henry, pleaded with the entire nation to "stop allowing evil to take over our bodies, our minds, our hearts, and our souls, because Judgment Day is fast approaching and we don't have much time"; he had seen in a dream the horsemen of the Apocalypse. Catholics, Anglicans, Hindus, and Muslims all called for a national day of prayer. The government promised more policemen on the streets, help from the army, and even more help from Venezuela's Guardia Nacional to patrol "our drug-infested waters." Alice and Scott had even discussed leaving the island, but they didn't want to end up in Miami like so many of their friends.

The phone rang. Alice heard Scott pick it up downstairs. After the call he came upstairs and gently shut the door of their bedroom. Alice glanced at the clock on the bedside table; it was already 2:35 p.m.

"That was Jeffery on the phone. They're not coming, Kathy is too upset. Apparently they tried to take the Clarke boy early yesterday morning, around three a.m. They followed him from the club. When he slowed down at the traffic lights before the turnoff into Golf View, they tried to grab him and push him into a car . . ."

"So what does that have to do with not bringing Charlotte?"

"Kathy is worried."

"About what?"

"I just said *what*—they nearly took the Clarke boy."

"So what does that have to do with Charlotte coming to Emma's party?"

"I don't know, the Clarkes live on the same street, quite close to them."

"I know all that but I still don't see what it has to do with Charlotte. Kathy is so damn jealous of everything. What does she think? That they going to take her? Or her lovely Charlotte? She thinks that they're really in the same league as the Clarkes?"

Scott kept silent, stared at her for a moment, then went into their bathroom. Alice heard the swish of the sliding door, then the shower. She sat down on her bed, then stretched out on a cushion and stared at the wooden rafters above. It had begun. The party was beginning to unravel; all that planning and now Emma would be disappointed. It was no secret that Kathy and Alice didn't like each other. Alice found that Kathy was superficial, snotty, and stupid. And it didn't help that Kathy's family had always been friendly with Scott's family, or that Alice felt that Scott's mother would have preferred Kathy for Scott, or that Kathy was undeniably pretty in that obvious sort of way. And the fact that Scott had spent those two nights at Jeffrey and Kathy's house when things were at their worst made Alice hate Kathy even more, because now Kathy probably knew about the affair although Scott swore he never told her. Once, early in their marriage, Scott told Alice that maybe she was just a little jealous of Kathy; after that, Alice didn't talk to Scott for a week, so now Scott avoided talking about Kathy unless, like today, it was unavoidable.

Scott got out of the shower, put on his jeans, white polo shirt, and a pair of sneakers. He left Alice still lying on the bed staring at the ceiling. He knew better than to say anything more about Kathy. Things seemed to be getting worse, not better; he didn't know how to talk to her anymore, so he usually agreed with her or said very little. He could see them moving away from each other in slow motion, like two people in a corny Bollywood film; he had been looking at this film for a while and now he had no idea how to get the two people back to that point close to the beginning where they seemed happy.

Alice watched Scott leave the room without saying a word. She could hear the dogs barking at Eric and William. She could even hear Emma's sweet giggle. But Alice, still smelling of curry, was tired, very tired. So she closed her eyes for what seemed like seconds; when she heard the buzzer for the gate it startled her; she had dropped off to sleep. She got up and walked to her bedroom window. It was Mr. Xavier with the horse for the party. The gate opened. She watched old Mr. Xavier get back into his rickety pickup, pulling the horse in another tray, and slowly drive up to the house. Scott and Ricky were already there to help him.

Suddenly she had the terrible thought of no children turning up for the party. But they would come; many had already RSVP'd; it was just Charlotte's absence and Kathy's desire to ruin everything, just to spite her, that troubled her now. Alice didn't want to think about the Clarke boy. Two young children had been kidnapped in the last month; the first had been tortured and beaten to death with a cricket bat, but he was the grandson of a well-known drug runner; the second child, a casino owner's son, again with a potential drug link, was simply shot in the head and had his hands cut off, a sign, the newspapers said, that the family had owed or stolen money. Both children, as horrible as their deaths were, came from what everyone called the "drug coast." But the Clarkes, they all knew the Clarkes; they were a wealthy family, quietly so; they owned some of the most beautiful property on the island, bought for a song by Grandpa Clarke long before anyone imagined that those areas would ever be worth anything or be populated. The Clarkes were rich but not from drugs. No one was immune anymore, not from this plague that seemed to be spreading so fast.

Faster than even Alice had expected. Last week on Alice's way home after picking up Emma from her school, she thought she was being followed by a black sedan with at least four heads in it; the car followed her from the moment she turned onto the main road all the way onto the main valley road. Alice wanted to call Scott on her cell phone but Emma was in the car and she didn't want to scare her. So she drove, pretending to listen to a new song Emma had been taught at school, and tried her best to keep an eye on the black car following her. As she passed the Pastora Valley police station she slowed down. Emma asked why, but Alice told her that she just wanted to give Sergeant Socks an invitation to her birthday party. As soon as she turned into the police station, the black sedan zoomed ahead. The policemen on duty told her that Sergeant Socks was out on a "recon." She left the invitation for Socks and drove away. Everyone in the vale invited Socks to their parties since they all depended on his goodwill to keep, as Socks said, "evil at bay."

In fact, with each month Socks was becoming more and more famous, not just for catching kidnappers or finding ganja fields all over the island, but recently for his cocaine discoveries. Only last week Socks and his men had found packs of cocaine brought in with the tide onto a beach in a remote fishing village on the north coast, the drug coast. The minister of national security and Socks were featured together on the front page of the *Daily News* after that incredible find; the minister was quoted as saying that the country needed more policemen like Socks: "We Need More Socks!" the headline read. Some months ago another newspaper hinted at a different side to Socks, suggesting police brutality, strong ties to the drug world, and questioned how he was able to find all those marijuana fields. But questions on the island were never pursued; it didn't matter which government party was in power. The last time Alice had seen Socks he was talking to a neighbour at the front gate; the Hernandezes had had a break-in while vacationing in London. Socks was his usual animated self, arms flailing and gesturing as he usually did with his thumb cocked and index finger pointed like a gun.

It was 3:20 p.m. Alice didn't want to get up. Her tiredness never seemed to leave her now; it was always there like the heat and the ashes in this never-ending dry season. But she knew it was more than tiredness; a feeling of deadness had taken over in the last couple of months, which made it harder to do the things she had managed to do before: taking care of Emma, going for a walk, pulling up weeds in the garden, calling a friend. She didn't feel like going downstairs to greet the guests, she didn't feel like going to her own daughter's birthday party. On the outside she pretended to worry about the details, the little things, but inside her head was filled with bigger worries: the shootings in the hills, the abused children on the front pages of the newspapers, the kidnapped bodies found lying in gutters, the disease-ridden prisons, the police beatings, the street children, the skeletal beggars, and everything Scott had taken away from her. Alice could not imagine a change, not in herself and especially not in this place she called home. She wanted to leave her life, the beautiful house, the valley; she wanted to sleep, but instead she got up, dressed, washed her face, brushed her hair, put on lipstick, mascara, perfume, and went downstairs before the first guest for the party arrived.

GHOST STORY

BY Barbara Jenkins

Cascade

(Originally published in 2012)

I t used to have a petty thief where we living. His name is
Ghost. Of course his mother didn't christen him that—no
way can you look at a defenceless little baby and drop the
name Ghost on him just so, not same time you putting on
the maljo jet-bead bracelet to ward off the evil eye. It must be
the people who used to live here long-time who give him that
name. Maybe in the early days he used to come like a spirit
and nobody seeing him and he earn his name under those
circumstances, but since we know Ghost, he coming in broad
daylight and we seeing him, but is like the name stick.

Any day of the week, Sunday to Sunday, you seeing Ghost
walking up and down the narrow road that winding through
our little valley. People in car swishing by having to be careful not to bounce him because he walking in the middle of
the road and cars have to weave round him. Ghost wearing
boots, like discarded army boots, black heavy lace-up boots
and where you expect to see socks, you see very dark brown
stringy hairy calves leading up to ropy thighs with the wide
legs of khaki shorts flapping around. Holding up the shorts
is a wide black leather belt, also looking like army throw-
out stock. And that's it for clothes. Ghost always bareback,
back running with sweat, and he have a full, lumpy crocus
bag fling over one shoulder or across the whole two shoul-

der. In one hand he holding some kind a tool: a three-canal cutlass or a hoe or a grass-swiper, sometimes is only a long stick with a hook at the end. We used to wonder how come police don't ever stop Ghost to ask why he breaking the law walking around the place with bare sharp tools when honest gardeners wrap up they cutlass and thing in gazette paper to keep within the law. But is when you look at Ghost face you know why nobody don't stop him to ask no question, because Ghost face always set up vex-vex like he about to cuss you, he eye cokey and have a wild look, the raggedy beard and the thick-thick locks hanging in two-three dense clotted mat like a old coconut-fibre doormat. You feel anybody could put God out they thoughts to even say morning or evening when they pass him? Furthermore, if you do say something and he shake his head, is you self getting spray with the old sweat he harbouring in the beard and locks. Too besides, he striding up and down purposefully like he have somewhere to go and he can't be late and you fraid to get in his way, but most of all is because he looking don't-care, and don't-care is like untouchable to us ordinary people. But that don't mean people didn't talk to Ghost at all. We used to have plenty conversation with Ghost—after all, is only good manners to exchange a few words with a person who spending more time in your yard than you.

Everyone in our suburban area of houses scrambling along the face of the steep hill slope have a favourite Ghost story. When we meet up at one another house for breakfast after church on a Sunday morning, was always a chorus of complaints about Ghost. Marjorie say one time she hearing the dogs barking and she gone outside to check. The dogs and them running around and around a orange tree and she look up and see Ghost. She say, What you doing there? He say, I picking some orange. She say, Get down, get down at once, and he get down. She tell him, When you want something, you must ask for it. And she tell him to get out her yard. Next morning, she hear someone calling, Morning, ma'am, morning, ma'am, at the gate. Marjorie in the middle of preparing breakfast buljol, but she go outside. Is Ghost. I come for some orange, he say. She say, Okay, and she lead him to one of the tree. Pick from this one, she instruct. Ghost shake his locks. Not that one, he say. Them orange too sour. I taking from that one over there. Them sweeter. He pick and pick and when he done he tell Marjorie, Look, I pick some for you too, and he leave about a dozen or so in the mop bucket by the back step.

Hazel say she ketch Ghost in the zaboca tree and tell him to come down immediately. He say, I can't come down yet, I have a order to fill. Hazel tell us she understand, because that same afternoon she see the same zaboca self, now label avocadoes, at the nation's favourite grocery, for ten dollars each. When Nicky tell Sue that Ghost pick out all the nice yellow-flesh breadfruit and he tell her when she see him leaving the yard with the crocus bag bulging that he leave three more for her and they will be full enough to pick next week, Sue say, But he is a nice man, last week he sell me some really nice julie mangoes, five for ten dollars. Mavis say, He thief those mangoes from off my tree. Sue say, Your Julie is the best I eat this season. So it look like he harvest from the one and sell to the other, keeping the fruit circulating and making up deficiencies where he seeing them, like keeping a balance in nature or like supply-side economics, with him as middleman.

Louisa say, Is people like Ghost who keeping the neighbourhood safe because he always on the lookout, he know everybody times of day and comings and goings and if a strange bandit come in to do real harm, he will see them. She say, We

BARBARA JENKINS // 199

don't recognise that Ghost is our protection. Marlene laugh and say, We should call him Holy Ghost then. But Louisa quickly remind her blasphemy is a sin. Okay, sorry, Marlene agree, is like having a kind of informal security and we paying with surplus fruit. Is not surplus, Denise say, is years I watching my young zaboca tree. First year it bear, is only one zaboca, but it big and nice, smooth texture, dryish. Next year three fruit and I waiting for them to be really full before picking and one morning I look for them and they gone. That wasn't no surplus. He coulda pick one to sample for future reference and leave two for my family until the tree start to bear more. Is hard to have a tree in your own yard and have to buy zaboca in the grocery. People sympathise, yes, we agree, Ghost does be real indiscriminate sometimes.

But Ghost know everybody business and Maureen say he and her husband does talk good and make joke and only last week her husband pass Ghost sitting on the bridge, and her husband ask him when he think the zabocas will be ready and Ghost tell him, Boss, them zaboca have another three weeks still, and how Ghost really have a good heart because when her husband was sick Ghost look in the bedroom window and say, Boss, I hear you ent too well, look after yourself, eh? I go be real quiet. I ent go disturb you. Look, I going to shut your dogs in they kennel so they go stop the barking while I here. And then he proceed to pick off all the full limes. When Ghost leaving he see Debra coming in the gate. She hustling-hustling, because she had to drop the child by the child father mother as her own mother had to go out. Debra already late for work and she have to hurry up to start preparing lunch but he stopping her and telling her to bring out a bowl for him. She steupsing but she still bring it out for him. You know what he do? He put down the crocus bag and he drop a couple dozen or so limes in the bowl and he say, Make some juice for the boss, I don't find he looking too good, nuh.

Ghost and we woulda continue like that if the mealy bug hadn't arrive in a schooner-load of plantain and dasheen from Grenada. In a few months many of the fruit trees off which Ghost was making a living was infested and bearing less and less fruit; in a year, pickings was meagre. Ghost begin to use his intelligence of the area to supplement his income in a different way. Children bicycle left in the yard begin to disappear, Maureen wake up one morning to find the toolshed ransack and lawn mower missing, Denise hear what she thought was rain in the night then next day see pieces of PVC piping lying around spouting water and her six-hundred-gallon Roto-plastic water tank gone. Is now a different relationship start to develop between us people and Ghost. What we used to tolerate before as a kind of sharing was now theifing. If tree bear plenty, you can spare some, it cost nothing, next year it will bear again; but if you pay good money for something and it gone, you have to pay more good money to buy it back.

People start to lock gate, put up chain-link fence where they was depending on steep drop to be deterrent, some even put in automatic gate and a barrier came between Ghost and his host. He start to walk the street doing house-to-house visit, calling at the front gate, asking for work. He offering to do garden and clean yard, wash car and so on. Some people feel sorry and take him on but when you make arrangement for him to come Wednesday and you wait and wait for him and he ent come, you bound to get vex, and when he turn up Friday and say he had something else to do, you tell him don't bother, you will cut the grass yourself, or wash the car or whatever. It looking like Ghost life always too free for him to get tie down with day and time.

One Saturday morning, Denise pick up the papers from where the delivery man throw it in the yard and she see that a man in the next valley shoot a bandit who he see walking out his yard with his bush-whacker over his shoulder. The papers say the bandit was wounded in the back and was warded under observation in hospital. They print the bandit name: Alfred Thomas. Nobody didn't take it on, nobody think they know any Alfred Thomas, but when Debra come to work that morning she well excited. She calling from by the gate self, Miss Maureen, Miss Maureen, guess what? I hear Ghost get shoot. People was talking about it in the maxi coming up. Before you know it, is all of we people calling round to one another and saying how the Alfred Thomas in the papers is Ghost, and Sunday morning all of us by Maureen for breakfast and the subject is Ghost and the shooting and Maureen ask what we going to do about it.

Marlene say, What you mean what *we* going to do about it? What that thiefing rascal getting shoot have to do with *us*? Denise, still vex about the water tank and the zaboca, say, It damn good for him, now he will have to keep his blasted tail quiet. Hazel say, That is not a nice sentiment to express on a Sunday morning after coming from church. Denise say, If you did have something thief you woulda be damn vex too. Nicky say, Oh no, what I going to do now? And she say that she was expecting Ghost to come Monday to clean the yard, the drains slimy with moss, and now she would have to do it by herself and her back not feeling so good these days. Marjorie say that it is a good thing she wasn't depending on him for any yard work, and anyway, yes, she have to agree with Denise that Ghost get what he looking for long-long time. Mavis say, Poor feller, he don't deserve to get shoot for a bush-whacker when, right in the heart of government self, every manjack hand digging deep in the national cash register, and you don't see any citizen rushing out to do a citizen arrest or shoot any of them big thief. Sue say, Is people like you self that walk quite to the polling station and stain your finger for them. Is the people like you self put them in power; like all you people don't remember the track record they had build up when they was in government last time. For the people in this carnival-mentality country everything is a nine-days wonder. Mavis answer that the last lot wasn't no good either and like we head hard and can't learn no lesson from experience. Sue say, Mavis, you confusing the issue, who is big thief and feathering they own nest, giving big contract to friend and family is besides the point. Louisa say, Ladies, ladies, stop that please; don't bring no politics talk here today. The subject we discussing is Ghost, who lying wounded in a bed in the public hospital, and at least we could feel good that is not us who responsible for putting him where he is. She say, I asking all of you, who looking after Ghost interest now he get shoot? Ghost is somebody we know and he is a human being too and I personally don't see how we can let him just lie down there in the hospital, shoot-up, and nobody caring if he living or dead. Well, with that little sermon, we focus and we talk and talk and we agree somebody had to go on a mission of mercy and visit the hospital to check up on Ghost.

Debra serving out some guava juice at this point in the talk, and she volunteer to help out and go and see Ghost in hospital. She say she know about the public hospital, where the different wards is—male medical, male surgical, and so on. She say she know the rules and regulations about visiting time and number of visitors allowed and she say how we kinda people wouldn't know how to deal up with them security who like to rough up people who wearing church hat and talking and behaving hoity-toity. Denise want to take on the hoity-toity challenge Debra throw down just so, but Louisa jump in quick and say, Well, thank you, Debra, that's very kind, we appreciate your offer. Everybody agree that Debra is the most suitable person of all of us to tackle the petty bureaucracy of government-run space.

That same afternoon self, Debra set out with a bag of mango, orange, and sapodilla we gather up hurry-hurry, to visit Ghost and take him our get-well-soon message. When she come back Monday morning she say, Ghost not doing too good, nah: the bullet still inside and he have to have operation. Well, things start to get technical now and is like we have to intervene beyond mango and sapodilla. We send back Debra next day; she don't mind, she getting off work early and her role now enhance beyond cooking and cleaning: she is the designated mediator. Her mission is to find out who is the doctor on the ward, when the operation is, whether police pressing charges, and so on.

Debra come back and say the operation is for next week Thursday if the theatre have current and if they get through the backlog from last Thursday when current gone whole day. She say she know the fellow who does make up the list for the surgeon and he say he could put Ghost name high up on the list if he get some encouragement for him and for the surgeon too. All-a-we vex like hell about this grease-palm business, what the hell the oil and gas royalties is for, what taxes is for, what else health surcharge is for if not to make everything in public hospital and public clinic available for everybody in the public, irregardless, and ent these people getting pay already, from we same tax, etc., but, after all said and done, all-a-we know is vent we only venting; we know this is not a whistle to blow so easy, when people out there in the know have it to say that even the head of the district hospital authority been seen to be redirecting brand-new hospital equipment and supplies the Health Ministry pay good money for, to his own private clinic. We not powerful but we not stupid; we know the cards stack in their favour not our own and if we play mad and say we going public about corrupt practice, before you could say bribery and corruption, Ghost would be discharge immediately with the bullet still inside him and then what we will do? Paying the same surgeon to do the operation in his private clinic was out of the question. So we agree to shut up, sub up, and help out; it will be cheaper in the long run. Eventually talk done and everybody boil down and agree and pull out wallet and purse, cash only, no cheque.

Debra continue to visit in the hospital, Ghost get the operation, Ghost discharge, Ghost home recuperating. And Debra bringing us the latest news about how Ghost progressing. That he living up a steep hill over by so, with a dirt track to the house Ghost and his father scramble to build together. And that now that his father dead, is his mother and sister living there with the sister three children. That the sister does do a little hairdressing—braiding, weaving, straightening—and how she expand to nails too with her biggest girlchild helping out, learning the same beautician business because it does pay good, because everybody want to look nice, and that the school the same girlchild pass for is only a waste-a-time place, the teachers don't come to class and the children only having sex in the classroom and taking videos with they cell phone and sending it all around the place and some even selling it on the Internet, and how she don't want her daughter mixing up in that kind a thing, is best she help out with the business and learn something she could make a living with. Debra say to us, All you don't have to study Ghost at all, nah, he mother and sister helping he out. We self wondering among ourself, but of course not out loud in front of Debra, how come poor people does have enough money for hairdos but only buying Crix biscuits and Chubby sweetdrink for they children when the day come, and how come little-little schoolchildren can have cell phone with camera in it and not have books for school, but, in the end, we exhaling, we well glad that it looking like Ghost pulling through all right. So we listen to Debra and we lay Ghost to rest for the time being as we have plenty other thing to deal-up with.

Outside in the yard, we seeing that the mealy bug finally ecologically controlled by a fast-multiplying ladybird colony they bring in from India and fruit trees flowering good again. Mangoes ripening and falling in the yard and rottening, zabocas too high in the tree for we older folks to pick; is only iguana and manicou enjoying the fruit. Nowadays gardener and them don't want to climb no tree for you. They only coming in a team, cutting lawn *zrrr, zrrr, zrrr* with the whacker, blowing grass cuttings *vroom, vroom* and then gone, quick-quick to the next yard, and you standing there like a fool with your purse empty, and nothing you really want do getting done.

One Sunday morning Maureen hear people calling, Morning! Morning! at the gate and she look out the kitchen window. She see two neat and tidy people, a man and a woman. The woman wearing a floral-print shirt-waist dress, white sandals, a white hat, carrying a straw basket in one hand and holding a pink parasol in the other. The man in a long-sleeve white shirt, blue tie, black soft pants, and black lace-up shoes, black parasol. Maureen wondering what they could be selling and she go to the gate and she see the man holding a big maco Bible and the woman basket have magazine in it. They say,

Good morning, madam, and we are messengers of the Lord coming to bring you blessings from Jesus.

Maureen tell us afterwards she feel something was familiar but she couldn't say exactly what until the man say, Miss Edwards, you don't remember me? Alfred Thomas. She say the name sounding familiar but where she know him from? The man say, I used to get lime and zaboca from your yard. She say she look at him good-good. And in the eyes and the eyes alone, she recognise Ghost. His hair cut flat down to his scalp, his face clean-clean; she say is the first time she see he have forehead, ears, cheeks, chin like everybody else. She say she didn't say the name Ghost out loud because maybe the woman didn't know about his past and it wasn't her business to reveal nothing, so she just say, Oh yes, is you, Alfred, I didn't recognise you. He say, I seen The Light, Miss Edwards. Jesus reach out to me and save me. I was in hospital and a pastor come and show me I was on the wrong path. He point me in the right direction and now I am save. Miss Edwards, I want you to be save too and everybody I uses to know. You have a few minutes to spare for the Lord and Saviour Jesus Christ? Maureen say she didn't know what to say. She had time for the Lord and Saviour Jesus Christ, yes, of course, but she didn't have no time for Ghost, now known as Alfred Thomas. So she say she have food on the stove and maybe another time when she wasn't so busy. He give her a magazine and the two of them gone up the hill by where Denise and Mavis living.

Every Sunday Alfred and a lady at the gate, sometimes the same lady as first time, sometimes a different one, but always is Alfred. And every Sunday people hiding and making excuse not to go out by they gate and fight-up with Alfred attempt at religious conversion: they just about to go and bathe, they have plantain frying and can't leave the stove, they on a phone call to they daughter in foreign. We don't really care for the evasiveness but the man become a absolute botheration. And whole week-a-day, we people raking up and sweeping up and piling up whole heap a rotten mango and carcass of hollowed-out zaboca skin and seed that drop when the iguana and parrot done with them and we wondering how after one-time-is-two-time and how you never appreciate what you have until it done. And in the middle of all the grumbling and all the what to do, you know, is Debra self who again pull us out of this stalemate situation.

One Sunday, Maureen gone out to man the cake stall at the church bazaar, and when the two proselytizer come by the gate, Alfred lady ask if she could use the bathroom, please, so Debra let the two-a-them come in. Alfred and Debra waiting in the gallery for Alfred lady to finish her business in the bathroom when Alfred spot the julie mango tree laden with fruit. He ask Debra who does pick it. Debra say, Well, where the picker pole could reach they get pick, but plenty too high to reach. Alfred say, Tell Miss Edwards I coming Tuesday to help out.

So said, so done; Tuesday morning bright and early Alfred at the gate. Debra had already tell Maureen what Alfred say but Maureen say she will wait to see with her own two eye before she believing anything Ghost say. Alfred tell Maureen he come to help pick the mango and she let him in. Well, he pick and pick and full up a whole crocus bag. He tell Maureen the day work come to two hundred dollars. Maureen pay him, then she and Debra had to go and share mango through the whole neighbourhood, because how much mango one person could eat, eh? Is a setta work to pulp and juice and freeze, and who have freezer big enough to pack-up with a setta mango pulp? You tell me. Hazel pay him two hundred dollars the following week to pick out her zabocas and he buy back most of what he pick for a hundred dollars and take the bag with him. He say he have an order to supply the little street-side vegetable stalls. And so it went with the pootegal, the orange, the sapodilla, the pommecythere, and the grapefruit. People find theyself paying Alfred to do what Ghost use to do for free.

One day, Alfred come to Maureen yard and he find a big truck park-up in the yard. It mark *Green Fingers Tree Removal Service*. He hearing *brrz, brzzz, brrrzzzz*. When he look, he see two big man with a chain saw cutting down the pomerac tree, branch by branch from the bottom branch. He rush for the man holding the saw and start to pelt cuff. The man drop the saw and it start to race around by itself in circles till the next man catch it and turn it off. What you think you doing? Alfred challenge the man. The man say, The lady here call us to cut down the trees. Maureen, hearing the saw stop and hearing the commotion, come out to investigate. She explain to Alfred that she cutting down all the fruit trees because it now a nuisance to have them: too expensive to upkeep, too much waste, too much mess in the yard with leaves and fallen fruit. She add that furthermore, from now on she buying what she want from the grocery. Alfred sit down right there on the ground between all the leaf and branch and the red star-spatter of buss-up pomerac and start to bawl like a little child who get plenty licks. How you could do a thing like that? he say. You don't know how much a people all over the place depending on them pomerac and sapodilla and mango. You have any idea what them fruits and them does mean to people like we? Is how long I know all you? Why we can't talk about this man-to-man like two big people? Maureen tell the tree-cutting men to stop a minute while she has a quiet word with Alfred. The two of them go to the gallery and sit down and talk. Debra bring out some lime juice for the both of them and they talk some more. When Maureen come back outside, she tell the cutting crew to go back to the company; she don't need them and she will call the office and settle up.

Since then, Louisa finding two big hand a green fig by the back steps and when she check, the big bunch that was hanging down on the fig tree down the slope gone. Denise mop bucket always have a few lime or pootegal and orange when they in season and the tree and them still have some left back. Most morning, Nicky finding a nearly ripe zaboca on the kitchen window sill and no rotten ones on the ground. And Mavis enjoying not only julie but starch and graham mango with no flies and rotten fruit under her julie tree. If Maureen husband forgetting to close the gate at night, Maureen not making no fuss with him, and when two chain-link post with ten feet of link wire at the back by Denise lose they footing and slip down in a little landslide in the rainy season, nobody bothering to put it back up.

When we ladies meeting for Sunday after-church break-fast, some wit may remark to the hostess that she enjoying the nice homemade pommecythere jam but where you hiding the pommecythere tree, girl? And a next time, a person may wink when she complimenting on a sweet mango nectar at the home of someone who can't boast of a mango tree, and all the rest of us smiling-smiling, because we figuring that is really like a Ghost does be passing through in the night.

THE DRAGONFLY'S TALE

by Sharon Millar

Northern Range

(Originally published in 2013)

Carmelita

Weeks before Christmas, in the hills of the Northern Range, a boy disappears from home. He is seventeen years old. His mother, Carmelita Nunes, calls on the Orisha gods and prays to St. Anthony, the patron saint of lost things. Her son is not yet a man and she knows that makes him both more dangerous and more vulnerable. On the first day of his absence, she draws a thick black line through the almanac hanging on the kitchen wall. On the third day, a black Friday, she dresses in her best clothes and calls a taxi. When she passes through the village, sitting in the backseat, some people raise their hands in gentle waves while others stare, their arms still. The village had lost hunting dogs and caged parrots, but never a boy. Even the aging white French Creole, who has never spoken to her, and old man Lum Fatt, who still dreams of China, come to see her drive down the winding road toward the police station.

Carmelita is not naive, but weeks before, when her two other children had come to the house to talk about Daniel, she'd turned her head and raised the volume on the radio. First Oriana had come and then Johnny. It was only after Daniel had raised his hand to her, the hand moving from his side with lightning violence, that there was talk of sending him to

Johnny in town. "Send him," Oriana had said, "send him so that Johnny could teach him about respect." He'd stayed with Johnny and his wife for less than two days. *Oh God*, Carmelita thought, after Johnny called to say Daniel was heading home.

"You can't talk some sense into him?" Her voice echoed down the telephone wire.

"I have Lilla to think of, Ma. She's afraid of him."

Most of the young boys make their money growing weed in the forest, ducking and hiding from the police helicopters that swoop like clumsy dragonflies before chop-chopping their way back to the city. *That's all it was*, she thought, *nothing the other boys aren't doing.*

To keep him at home, Carmelita showed him how to curry birds: chickens, ducks, pigeons. Cutting, chopping, frying, stewing. She held a plucked duck over the open fire, singeing the skin, cut the fat gland off the end of a chicken, and killed a pigeon quietly without breaking its tiny bones. She showed him how to add pimento pepper and ground ginger as her mother had taught her.

"South boys work in oil and town boys work in banks," said Daniel as he watched her cook, "but what happen to the village boys from the north?" He spoke to the duck, sitting cold and pimple-skinned on the counter, not to her.

"You think any tomato or christophene could ever compete with that black gold? Those south boys born into that. It come like they own that fountain of oil. And town boys only eating sushi and managing money market."

The duck was now in the pot, its skin sizzling and browning, mixing with the seasoning, flooding the kitchen with such a good scent that it was as if he were saying something that she wanted to hear, something happy. When she looked up from the pot, his topaz eyes were on her, baleful and sly. She tamped down the doubt that she'd grown this child. Looking away, he shook his head, a quick movement, like a dog trying to get water out of his ear.

Later, he told her that sometimes they worked from a small base on Chachachacare, the abandoned island that once housed nuns and lepers—he'd seen women, dark silhouettes on the pirogues. "They'll kill me if they know I talk," he told her later that night. "They tell me so all the time."

"Who is *they*, Daniel?" she asked. "Who is *they*?"

But he was too busy eating his duck to answer her.

That night she looked up the word *sushi* in the dictionary, but it was not listed in her old pocket version. Though she did find the word *cocaine*.

It is only after they pass the large immortelle tree, the big taxi juddering into first gear on the hairpin turn, that Carmelita allows herself to breathe. Now that she is out of view, she can stop feeling shame. No doubt the villagers will have milled around in the road after she left, looking for the silvery flashes of the big Chevrolet as it rounded the corners of the hill.

Mr. Ali is only called up to the village in emergencies. Right next to her on the backseat is the faint brown stain from when Myrtle nearly sliced off her finger and Carmelita had to hold her hand up over her head while Mr. Ali barrelled down the hill. Myrtle is a good friend; thirty years of looking at each other across a hedge, day and night, and minding each other's children, made them like family. Myrtle had come over last night to tell her the village talk.

"People saying that Dan cross Chale Jamiah," she said. "Is one of two things happen to him, Carmelita. Either Jamiah's people pick him up or the police hold him. The only thing we could do is pray."

Carmelita had run this conversation over and over in her mind all night. She'd played it like a movie, each word an image. Everyone knew Chale Jamiah grew tomatoes. No one dared to say that tomatoes couldn't build that big house in town; there was even talk that he'd bought an oil rig. You could sell tomatoes from morning to night but even the simplest child could do the math. Tomatoes didn't buy oil rigs. He was a big whistler as well. They said he could whistle any tune. A nice-looking man who whistled and grew tomatoes. She'd met Jamiah once years ago when he'd come to the house to pay his respects after Frank had died. "Farmer to farmer," he'd said, and she hadn't thought any more of it.

When Frank collapsed in the lettuce bed at the side of the house, Carmelita was soaping baby Daniel's head, shielding his golden eyes, he chittering in the lukewarm water of his kitchen-sink bath, little happy chirrups of contentment as the water poured over his head. She'd run to go to Frank, leaving Daniel in the water, wailing and slippery. By the time Mr. Ali made it up the hill, Myrtle had covered Frank's face with a flowered sheet. After this Carmelita began to pray, imagining her prayers carrying the soul of her husband. She'd picked roses for Mother Mary while keeping her eyes open for five-toed hens to woo the Orisha gods. On some nights she'd burned incense for Ganesh who shared a shrine with Jesus under the hog plum tree. She wasn't taking chances with Frank's soul.

In the town below, Mr. Ali lets her out into a river of heated bodies—people swimming like guabines on the pavement. On the main boulevard, Guyanese and various small-island immigrants hock their wares. Cheap panties and pirated DVDs, strung side by side on collapsible display racks, hover above dirty drain water. At the police station, she looks for Corporal Beaubrun, a distant cousin.

He's in the middle of breakfast, smoked herring and bake on his desk. Wiping his hands on the seat of his pants, he comes toward her. He's a good-looking boy. Tall and dark with a square head and a nose carved like an answer to his heavy brow. At the counter he takes his time pulling his pen out of his pocket.

"I hear you having some trouble with your last one," he says.

"He misses a father's hand."

"How long has he been gone?"

"Since Wednesday morning. He said he was coming down here to do some business."

"He wasn't in school?"

She shakes her head.

"He has a woman?"

"No." *Oh God*, she thinks to herself, *is this man so dense that he does not understand what I am asking of him?* "It might be too late when you all finally decide to look for him," she says carefully.

"You know something you not telling me?"

"No, just worried."

He shuffles a few papers on his desk. "How long we know each other?"

"Since primary school, you know that. What's that got to do with this?"

"Sit tight and he will come home. The more trouble you make—"

"To look for a missing child is to make trouble?"

He places the cap back on his pen and glances at his breakfast. "Come," he says. "Come and talk outside. I'll walk you out."

They leave the station, his hand lightly on her elbow.

"Has he ever told you who he works for?" He explains that the boys are recruited from villages all over the island. They are well paid to do what they consider easy work. These rural boys know the terrain, the trails through the hills, and are handy with their homemade pipe-guns. They are routinely moved around the island to fill gaps in an army of small-time criminals. If Daniel is ambitious and bright, could he be involved in this?

Carmelita hesitates before answering. What can she say without implicating her son in wrongdoing? Can she believe her youngest son knows right from wrong? Has she been too indulgent with him? She shrugs her shoulders. "Maybe. I can't say for sure."

Beaubrun sighs and pulls a handkerchief out of his back pocket to wipe his brow. "I'll call you if I hear anything. I'll make some enquiries."

All day she walks. She passes the old cathedral, cavernous and violet, which stands next to De Freitas Dry Goods with its bags of coffee, cocoa and nutmeg, pigtail buckets, and piles of blue soap. At the end of the street, Chan's Laundry puffs little blasts of starchy steam onto the pavement. In this part of town, blue-bitch stone faces the fronts of the buildings, the corners laid with old ships' ballast. Her father laid blue-bitch all his life—that hard beautiful stone pulled from the earth below the village—a solid, honest life, he always told his children. Work from the land.

She has a picture of Daniel in her hand, holding it up toward the faces of strangers who sidestep her. When the sun begins throwing long shadows, Carmelita veers off the main street, crossing the river that leads to the other side of town. On this side, drinking men spill out from shanty bars with their nasty, stale urine and rum-sweat smells. Alleys dribble off the main road, wildness taking over. Behind the derelict government housing, the grid-order of the town disappears into indeterminate ends, twisted mazes of collapsing galvanized sheets and open latrines. Here and there golden marigolds grow in discarded truck tires. Farther on are the monstrous yards of the scrap-iron vendors, rumoured to be the front offices of bustling rent-a-gun operations. Surely someone here must know him. Recognize his face. Tell her something that the police could not.

Down an alley, in the dim light between the buildings, two women sit on an overturned Coca-Cola case with a makeshift table between them. One, a coarse-skinned Indian woman, is picking out seeds and leaves from a pile of weed, separating it into neat heaps. The second one looks up as Carmelita approaches, her hand motionless over the line of weed on the cigarillo paper. Both women shift at the same time, perfectly synchronised, blocking her view of the table.

"How do you do business?" she whispers. *Is it like chicken*, she wonders, *that you buy by the pound?*

The older woman holds up a finger to Carmelita. *Wait*, she is clearly saying. *Don't come any closer*. She rises heavily, wearily, rubbing her back as she comes toward Carmelita.

"Do you know him?" Carmelita shows her the picture.

"How much you want?"

"Ahhm, one."

"Just give me a twenty." The woman takes the photograph from Carmelita. "Why you looking for this boy?"

"I'm his mother. He's missing."

"Everybody down here know Daniel." The woman makes the sign of the cross before bagging the joint.

"When last you saw him?"

Before the end of the street, she's thrown the joint into a clump of bushes.

When the sun cools she walks home. She stays off the pitch, still radiating the day's heat, walking in the grass at the side of the road, her breath loud in her ears as she climbs and climbs up to her village. Halfway up, her feet stinging from the tiny pebbles on the road, she stops. The plateau overlooks the Gulf of Paria, a big, broody expanse of water. People say that this is where the cocaine crosses, coming from Venezuela. Across the bay, South America is just visible in the dying light. The scarlet ibis are flying home. They fly across the indigo water heading inland toward the swamp. Years before she'd taken Daniel to see the pink birds roost. The birds had landed in rosy blurs, whole ibis families staining the mangroves red.

"Mama, how do they know to come here every night?" he'd asked.

"They come," she'd told him, "because this is where they sleep. Even the littlest bird knows he must come home to his mama."

When she catches her breath, she begins walking again.

"Don't cry," says Myrtle the next morning when she brings Carmelita the newspapers and a ball of cocoa. "Daniel too beautiful to die. He'll be alright. Don't cry, Carmelita."

A lagniappe child, the villagers said when her stomach began to rise like bread with Daniel. She was forty-four then. A change-of-life baby will break your heart, the old midwife told her. Two months before his due date, Daniel was born in a tropical storm. He was her smallest baby but she'd had the worst time with him. She had all the others at the hospital but Daniel was born in her bed, bloody and breathless.

Against her thigh, his skull was no larger than a monkey's, his skin translucent under the hurricane lanterns. The midwife wrapped him in a blanket and placed him in the drawer of a dresser. Carmelita had softened the edges of the drawer with cotton padding laid over sweet-smelling vetiver sprigs. For the first month of his life he wore a bracelet of black beads on his tiny wrist to ward off maljeaux while she prayed to keep the breath in his body. The baby had nothing of her flat, wide face and hairless sapodilla skin, or his father's smooth cocoa complexion. He was thin-faced with marmalade eyes, a beautiful changeling child.

Father Duncan comes right behind Myrtle early on Saturday morning. Daniel has been gone three mornings. Four nights her son has slept somewhere else and she has no idea where. The night before, she'd not slept well, her feet aching from the long walk up the hill, and she rose twice to the sound of a baby's cry. But each time it was only the big jumbie bird, roosting in the mango vert tree up behind the house. By the time she waves Myrtle out the gate and turns to go back inside, Father Duncan is already striding up her path, as if tragedy has made him lose his manners, his crucifix glinting in the sun, his great head bobbing above the scarlet flowers of the hibiscus hedge. She has to hide Ganesh, snatching him from beside Jesus, pushing his elephant head deep in the compost heap. But in the end, she is happy the priest has come and they say the rosary together, pausing after each decade to allow the words to drift up to Mary's ears.

Beaubrun telephones on Monday morning.

"A body of a young boy was picked up by the Caura River. They've sent him to the mortuary in town. That's all I know."

Her heart beats a galloping staccato that rushes in her ears and brings black spots before her eyes. The telephone falls from her hand and hits the statue of Mary, knocking the mother of God off her pedestal and narrowly missing the Sacred Heart with the bloody heart of Jesus popping out of his chest. Carmelita opens her mouth and bawls.

Afterward she remembers that the village poured through her door like red ants, laying their hands on her, but even the softest touch bit and stung her skin and made her scream. It was only when old Dr. Chin arrived in his Honda CR-V to stick a needle into her arm that Carmelita stopped screaming.

On Tuesday morning she packs a small bag to go to the mortuary. In it is a rosary, a bottle of holy water, a clean shirt, and an ironed pair of pants for Daniel. Mr. Ali comes when she calls, holding her elbow as she walks to the car as if she is an old woman.

"You don't have to go with Mr. Ali, Ma," Johnny had said, "I'll take you."

But she had told him no. This was about her and Daniel.

The old colonial-built hospital is filled with airy rooms that filter the trade winds; the view through the jalousies looks down on vendors selling colas and fruit drinks at the entrance. At the back of the hospital, the mortuary stares at Carmelita, its closed windows giving it a stupid, blind appearance. Inside, a small Indian woman listens to Carmelita's story before picking up the telephone. As she speaks, a small extra finger swings gently from the side of her left hand. This infant finger with its own half-moon nail causes a somersaulting in Carmelita's stomach, a clenching in her womb. Across the room a wooden door bears a nameplate: *Dr. Andrew Olivierre, Chief Patholo-*

gist. She takes a seat on a wooden bench across from this door.

"You can go in now," the secretary eventually says.

Dr. Olivierre comes to meet her as she walks through the door, holding out his hand and smiling pleasantly. "I'm sorry," he says. "There has been a mistake. I'm so sorry, Mrs. Nunes."

"Excuse me? The police sent me."

"We've seen this happen. People come in thinking they will find missing people here. But your son is not here."

They sit in silence for a moment or two. There is a picture of a pretty woman with three children on his desk. The woman looks like her daughter Oriana, same dark hair and wide mouth. The doctor has two daughters and a son. The oldest girl looks a little younger than Daniel and there is a baby in the woman's arms. The doctor flips his pen between his fingers and snaps it open and shut with sharp clicking noises.

"How you lose someone?" she asks the room. "A boy is not a handbag. Or a scrap of paper that fly off a table and disappear in the breeze; a boy is not something you could lose so."

"I'm so sorry for your loss, Mrs. Nunes," the doctor says, his hand resting lightly between her shoulders as she leaves the room.

She waits on the bench outside the hospital for Johnny to come and get her. She still has the bag of Daniel's clothes and the small bottle of holy water.

That night she dreams that Father Duncan caught a scarlet ibis and asked her to stew it for him to eat. The next morning, Wednesday, she draws a black line through the whole week on her almanac. She chooses a picture of Daniel sitting with the two dogs on her front porch. She will go back and give the doctor a picture. If Daniel does come in, at least he will recognize him.

When the car pulls into the mortuary the next morning, Carmelita is waiting. The doctor is in the passenger seat. The dark-haired woman from the picture kisses him goodbye, waving as he walks away.

"Goodbye," she calls.

The morning sun backlights the doctor's hair, but his face turns mulish and cruel as he approaches Carmelita. Still, she reaches out to touch him. When he clamps her wrist, she remembers how a dog bit her like this once, with a sudden snap.

"Your son is not here," he says, his big body, with its womanish bottom, stiff and hostile.

Behind him, the car stops, its engine idling, in the middle of the road. "Drew!" the woman calls.

Carmelita pulls her hand back, shaking her wrist, the photograph falling on the ground. When she looks up, he has walked away and the big car has driven off.

Drew

Drew carefully examined the body of the young boy. He had been brought in after midnight early Sunday morning. Blue and black discolourations of settling blood were just starting along the boy's back, his skin grey under the buzzing fluorescent lights. Tall, but still a child. No more than sixteen or seventeen. Could be a country boy, a cocoa panyol mixed with some Indian. There was a birthmark on his left cheek. Maybe a local white, but Drew doubted this because he'd know this child. Venezuelan? His mouth had collapsed into the spaces left by the missing front teeth, making the boy's face appear babyish. Drew turned up the top lip. The gums were bruised, puckering around little bloody pockets left by the extracted teeth. Drew ran his tongue over his own front teeth, a quick reflexive move. The ends of the boy's fingers had bled until death and now the hands curled lightly, peculiar and bird-like without their nails. Even with closed eyes, his face still had the startled expression of a panicked child as if the bullet had caught him negotiating to the end. A drug hit? But Drew knew that if Ralph had called him out, it meant the police were involved.

After he'd examined the body, Drew peeled his surgical gloves off, discarding them in the bin. The yellow death certificates came in triplicate, untidy with their bulging carbon copies. On the top copy, Drew carefully wrote the cause of death as *vehicular accident*. Underneath, he signed his name: *Dr. Andrew Olivierre, Chief Pathologist, St. Mary's General Hospital*.

The first bodies had begun arriving within weeks of the election. Last week there'd been a prostitute, a pretty girl who had tried to blackmail the wrong person. Was Ralph so powerful that he could arbitrarily order someone to be killed? Drew pulled the sheet up, covering the child's face. Where were this boy's parents? They were the ones to blame for this. He could put his head on a block that none of his three would ever end up like this. Irresponsible people having children had spawned a generation of feral teenagers. This is what the ruling party had said during the election campaign and the population had agreed so much that the party had swept into government on a landslide vote.

At his weekly confession, Drew had struggled with his conscience. What was he to say to the priest? That part of his job as the government pathologist was to make the victims of police brutality disappear? It was not as if he were associated with a death squad or anything like the Tonton Macoute in Haiti. This was simply some housecleaning to tidy up the streets. He turned off the lights, locked the door and left. It was 3:15 on Sunday morning. The boy had been dead for a little over twenty-four hours.

Ralph and Drew still met every Wednesday at the Cricket Club, even though Ralph was now a government minister. When they had turned up for lunch that first Wednesday after the election, the whole room had stood and clapped when Ralph entered. He looked like a minister of national security, as if everything in his life had been leading up to playing this part. Drew had held his briefcase while Ralph stopped to shake hands with people on the way to their table.

But today, no one looked up when they entered the room.

Drew cut his chicken carefully as he spoke. "The mother tried to stop me in the car park this morning. I told her we didn't have him. We should have buried him on Monday."

"Does anyone else know he was brought in?" asked Ralph.

"I should ask *you* that. This was a child. Shit, man. This is not what we're supposed to be doing."

"What a fuck-up. We didn't know he was so young." Ralph sipped his drink. "We think he double-crossed Jamiah."

"I still don't understand. Who killed the boy?"

"Our men did. He knew everything about Jamiah but he couldn't go back. We offered him protection to talk, but he refused."

"We can't be killing children."

"You know, the little shit never cracked. He never talked."

"They were very rough with him," said Drew. *This is where I should say something*, he thought, *this is where I should get up and walk out.*

"This boy doesn't exist anymore, so whoever *they* are could not have been rough with him. Do you understand? This boy must disappear completely. This was a fucking nightmare and now you giving me some crap to hold about this boy's mother? Make him disappear, Drew. It's your job."

No, Drew wanted to say, *it's not my job. This was not supposed to be part of it.*

"How long we go back, Drew? Come nah, man. How long we friends?"

I'd like you to be part of my team, Ralph had said. How many months ago? Was it six already? *If we want to clean up this country, we have to bend the rules a bit.*

He'd presented a convincing argument, but Drew had always known that he didn't have a choice.

In their final year at university, Drew had listened most nights to Ralph's low voice cajoling and stroking, the murmurs travelling through the walls. He couldn't believe the girls fell for it. But they did, every time. With a fleshy mouth that glistened pink and healthy when he laughed, a booming *ha-ha-ha* mouth that opened to show big, white teeth and a small, pointed tongue, Ralph was beautiful.

"It's not whether I like him or not—it's not about that. You can't resist Ralph, he's like a force of nature," Drew told Isobel when he first started seeing her.

"I can resist him," she'd replied.

"That's what all women say," he told her, but secretly he was pleased that she could see through Ralph.

Was this how it happened? That you crossed lines so easily? On their small island, where good and evil were so carefully demarcated, it was surprisingly easy to move between the two. Ralph was supported by a strong religious platform. It had been a clever manoeuvre by their prime minister to appeal to the righteous, a hard-nosed approach that sent shivers around the region. What was it the papers said? *An unprecedented show of military muscle.*

Every day, from the window in his office, Drew looked at the palms that waved the dead through, large branches forming a canopy against the sun. He was sorry that he had met with the boy's mother; sorry that she'd shown him the picture of the boy. In the photograph, an even-featured boy with odd topaz eyes had smiled out at him. White teeth set against copper skin, a saga-boy smile.

"Why do they keep calling you out at night?" Isobel had asked him on the way to work that morning. "Tell Ralph, when you have lunch with him today, that your wife wants to know why he keeps calling her husband in the middle of the night."

That night, after they'd made love, Isobel fell asleep with her back pressed up against him. She was sleeping deeply when he shook her awake.

"I have something to tell you," he said.

Isobel

The night Drew had woken her to tell her about the boy, there was no more lovemaking. She had to take a sleeping pill to fall asleep again. She woke groggy and waited for him to go to work before she got up. The hot water beating on her head when she showered cleared her thoughts. She would find the boy's mother and tell her the terrible thing her husband had done. She wore a comfortable pair of shoes; it would take an hour to walk to the hospital where she guessed the woman would be. Drew had taken the car that morning and he would be expecting her to stay at home.

She walked through the cows that grazed under the branches of the large saman trees. The passion fruit vine on the fence that separated their house from the banking complex was heavy with fragrant globes. She walked past the guava trees on the hillock that overlooked the houses of the rich on the coast. From here she could see the hospital on the other side of the savannah, up the street and left off the highway. She timed her breath to her stride, as if she were pacing herself for a long run. The road was quiet, the school rush over, her girls sitting safely in their classrooms; Robbie was having his morning fruit at his grandmother's home. Behind her, a truck roared up the highway, gears grinding as it picked up speed. She walked faster, trying to outpace the memory of Drew's face. He dropped the children at school every morning, letting her sleep because he knew she liked to read late into the night. He'd probably kept them quiet this morning, packing Robbie's bag and putting Mara's hair in a ponytail.

She broke into a short run, her breath labouring as the truck thundered past her, leaving her with a lungful of diesel fumes.

The woman was where she expected. She'd noticed her a few days before, the day she'd dropped Drew at work. She'd seen the violence in the way he'd grabbed the woman's hand. This had so shocked Isobel, she'd braked the car and called out to him. Now it made sense. And this was how she knew the woman would be here, sitting on a bench outside the mortuary.

"They have him," Isobel said when she sat down next to the boy's mother. "They have him inside. I'll come with you to get him. Come, we will go together." She was ready to face Drew. There was no need to tell the woman what had happened; she would be given a sealed casket. She told Carmelita to say that she would return with a lawyer if they did not produce her son.

Drew let them into his office, his face even. Had she expected something more dramatic, a scene perhaps, or some form of repentance? Instead, his quiet acquiescence frightened her. She'd been sure that she had the upper hand, but she'd underestimated him, and now it was she who was forced to consider her position. What had she gambled with this move, what must she be prepared to surrender?

"The casket is sealed," he told Carmelita. "These discrepancies are quite normal. We were due to call you today. I am so sorry for your loss."

Isobel was thrown by his poise, shocked by his ability to lie so easily. This shifting of gears revealed a stranger hidden inside her husband. When she was a child, she'd once slept the whole night with a garden lizard under the blanket. It had made her feel ill to think of the lizard heating up from her warmth.

"The casket will go to the funeral home," she heard him say. "I'm signing the papers to release the body to the funeral home. You can bury him from there."

When he came home that evening, they did not speak for three days. On the third night, he woke her in the middle of the night.

"Do you know what the fuck you have done?" he asked her. "Do you? You've put us all in danger."

"I don't want to know, Drew." She kept her face averted. How much was she prepared to give up? Her marriage? The lives of her children?

The next morning they went on as usual because neither could think of what else to do.

It was only later that Isobel was able to piece together what had happened. The woman had bribed the funeral director to release the casket to her.

Let me bring the boy home for a last night. Let me feed his spirit one last meal. Let me pack his bag for heaven.

This is what Isobel imagined Carmelita would have said to the funeral director. It's what she would have said.

Later Carmelita told her that she had bathed Daniel with lavender-scented water, sponging each laceration and examining every inch of his body. The next morning, she'd asked Father Duncan to reseal the coffin. In the family plot, he settled gently in the loamy dirt grown by generations of flesh and blood. That night, Carmelita found a gun hidden under some clothes in Daniel's room. There was no one that she could ask about the technicalities of a gun. It shot when she fired. She looked up the address of Dr. Andrew Olivierre. It took her less than a week to learn the man's routine.

It still surprised Isobel that neither child had mentioned the attack at the old house. In the aftermath, both girls had been calm. Carmelita had appeared just after midday. The neighbours said she sat there for most of the afternoon, waiting through a light drizzle under the trunk of a frangipani tree. When Drew pulled up to the gate, she moved quickly.

When she heard the first shots, Isobel ran toward the echo. By the time she arrived at the gate, Drew had Carmelita pinned against the car. With her arm twisted behind her back, her scapula stood in bold relief, like a broken wing.

Isobel pulled Drew off the keening woman, her hands frantic over his body, feeling for mortal wounds to explain the blood.

"Surface wounds," she told him. "It's okay. It's okay, Drew. It's just a pellet gun. It's just pellets." Isobel knew that old women who live in the hills knew how to deliver babies, brew raw medicine, and cook like angels, but they did not know how to use guns. The pellet gun had wobbled in her trembling hands.

"Why you lie? Why you lie about Daniel? You know they kill him. You see how they strip his body and rip it up like a old bedsheet. You see how they knock out his teeth and pull out his nails. I grow that child like a plant. From a seed, I grow him. Why you lie, Mr. Doctor? God don't sleep. You will rot in hell."

"Stop it," said Isobel. "Enough."

"Miss Isobel. Is his signature. His writing. He signed it. And he had to see what I saw. He knew. He knew what they did and he lied for them. Is pure evil. Pure evil your husband do that night."

That night Isobel and Drew made love for the first time since the day she'd appeared with Carmelita. At first they were cautious but soon they held each other with the sharp bites and blind thrusts of an unsettled argument. They were still very good together. But that morning she kept her face away, throwing an arm over her eyes and turning inward until he left the bed, not wanting to see the scabby marks on his chest.

By the end of the week they had moved to a quiet suburb and changed their phone numbers.

Isobel had never lived in the shadow of a mahogany tree. It stood tall, reaching toward the sky, giving off resinous clicks as it stretched its branches over the house. In the evening, the tree turned its leaves to catch the dry-season breeze that rode down the valley. If she listened from the kitchen, Isobel could hear the tiny pops as the tree released its cocoa-shaped pods, setting free the little helicopter spirals. Each morning she collected the spent husks where they lay curled like tiny sculptures on the sloping lawn that ran to the edge of the driveway.

The man who had lived there many years before had raised

hibiscus. People had driven from all corners of the island to choose from his rainbow-hued hybrids. It gave her pleasure to return hibiscus to the garden and tuck them neatly into fat manure beds that she shaped with her garden hoe.

Her new home was deceptive, modestly folding in on itself, presenting a bland facade to the road, but it came from a long pedigree of high-ceilinged, graceful houses that dotted the surrounding hills. It was not like the home of the man who lived across the street, a good-looking brown-skinned man they nicknamed The Whistler. His house was contemporary, bare-boned, dramatic.

Below their house was a damp cellar, secured with a temperamental padlock, where Isobel stored the baby bassinet with its elaborate netting and faint scent of vetiver. She had spent her first mornings in their new home in this cool dark cave rooting out hidden treasures from long-gone eras. All the while she hunted, she could hear her neighbour whistling his way through a catchy series of 1920s dance hits. She heard him sweeping his front steps as he whistled, a cheerful reassuring sound that reminded her of the nursery smell of boiling rice and butter. When she'd looked out from the cellar, all she could see was the smudge of his broom as it danced in a mist of sunlit dust motes. She'd heard that he was very rich, money made from growing tomatoes, according to the other neighbours.

Isobel and Drew seldom spoke of the incident at the old house. Now days were spent arranging new routines. Once she had built her world on the assumption that Drew was a good man. It was he who attended church with the three children every week. Her oldest, at eight, had just begun to question why Isobel came only infrequently to Mass. Ava was pretty and fine-boned, looking like Drew's mother, and the old lady shamelessly favoured her over the younger and plumper Mara. Her baby, Robert, was still beautiful in a bow-lipped, milky way. Everyone had told her that she would love the third child the most. When he emerged, perfectly whole and male, she feared he would steal her heart from her daughters. But her love for each child had a distinct flavour and texture, mercurial in the way it bubbled through her life.

The new house sat in the shadow of The Whistler's house. At certain times of day, the raw-boned house eclipsed their light, blocking the sun at its hottest point. Ralph had found the house for them after the shooting, though for a time there was talk about moving to Canada. Ralph said not to worry about Carmelita and they had not pressed charges. There would be no retribution and even if she did go to the police, she would not get far. Isobel made Drew promise that Ralph would not harm the old lady.

"It's the least you can do for her."

Ralph said he knew the neighbour, a nice man. He grew lots of tomatoes; he'd made his fortune in them. When she'd first heard him whistling, Isobel had thought about the boy. That day, on the bench outside the mortuary, Carmelita had told Isobel about Daniel. In his last months, Daniel had learned to whistle. He perfected the birdcalls of the Northern Range, practising the gong sound of the bellbird that lived high in the moist forest and whistling out the window at the jumbie bird in the mango tree. These were memories Carmelita wanted to keep.

It was good that Carmelita and Isobel never knew the bloody tune Daniel whistled until the end. Or how the soldiers in the forest had prepared the body of the child in the way they were taught by their elders. Brutal as they had been in life, they were gentle and superstitious in death, preparing the body with deference, worrying about the nine-night's ritual. Should they send a note to Dr. Drew to ask him to nail the boy's feet to the hastily assembled box that guilt made them build before they sent him to the mortuary? Should they insist that Dr. Drew bury the boy facedown so he could not come back for retribution? In their heavy uniforms, these men did not fear the living, but deep in the forest they would take no chances with a dead boy.

If Isobel had known these things, she might not have stayed. But she never knew any of this. Instead, in the dry rotting-leaf smell of her new garden, she learned how to skim unwelcome thoughts from the surface of her mind.

It was Mara who saw the dragonfly, a big blue darner among the red ones that gathered every evening to dance above the olive water of the pond. "Did you know," Isobel whispered, tickling the girls, "old wives say that he uses his tail to sew the lips of naughty boys shut? The devil's darning needles." They'd looked for him again, but he'd only come that once.

THE BONNAIRE
SILK COTTON TREE

BY SHANI MOOTOO

Foothills, Northern Range

(Originally published in 2015)

A t the beginning, or the end—one decides as necessary which is which—of every village on the island stands a lone silk cotton tree. *Woeful though it appears, its naked trunk towers above neighbouring trees. Above, its spread of branches houses birds, and at night bats rest there. Below, among the cavities in its massive buttressed roots, live some of the island's larger snakes. It is home, too, it has long been known, to restless duppies and the mischievous yet irascible jumbie.*

Note: In one of Trinidad's newspapers, an Irish priest named O'Leary writes a weekly column on things spiritual and religious. Father O'Leary frequently expounds on the proliferation of the dark arts of the Caribbean, no doubt in an attempt to draw the followers of such arts toward the church, and to discourage traffic in the opposite direction. From his newspaper-pulpit he has said that the Good Lord knoweth best and giveth in wisdom, while the jumbie gives—and yes, give he does—without judiciousness. The Good Lord, he says, guides His flock to know what is good and then to seek only such as is good to them and to others. But with jumbies, he admonishes, you must be careful what you ask for—for ask and ye shall surely receive, whether it is good for ye or not—because the jumbie gives only in exchange, and nine out of ten times he extracts from you more than you had imagined you'd pay—and do not for a minute doubt it: pay you must—the cost invariably including that you will bind yourself to a living hell. Father O'Leary does not realize, however, that his intentions have the reverse effect, and that church-, temple-, mosque-going people, and others with and without religious affiliations, all made desperately curious by his reports, have sought out the tree and its number one resident, each one imagining himself or herself to be that lucky one out of the ten.

Nandita Sharma was an artist, but unfortunately her medium was photography. In her recent solo exhibition at an art gallery in Port of Spain—timed to coincide with the free-spending mood of people at Carnival time—fifteen large framed photos were displayed. They were all colour still lifes of seafood. A close-up of a fish on the vendor's counter, its eye trained on the photographer. An extreme macro-shot of a bundle of tied crabs. Filling the entire plane of a thirty-two-inch square photograph, a single oyster was open, its meat bulging and glistening. Impaled on the upturned tines of a silver fork so highly polished its surface was a mirror reflecting the distorted image of the photographer was an almost transparent shrimp. Everyone who was anyone had come to the opening, and Nandita heard how technically masterful her photographs were, what a great eye she had, and that she should really do something with such talent. She was asked if she could come to someone's house and photograph the family, and if she was available to photograph someone else's mother's eightieth birthday celebration. Despite the compliments, not one of her photographs sold.

Family who had attended were dubiously proud. They

took her out to a restaurant after to celebrate, as her father put it in a toast to her, "the conclusion of that phase of your life and the hope that another is about to begin." Her father, owner of the largest newspaper on the island, said that they could finally see her potential in the field and offered to speak on her behalf with the paper's food editor about a job for her. She didn't mean to raise her voice against her father's offer, but the offer was evocative of all the reasons and incidents that had led her some years ago, at age twenty-seven, to let go of her place in her family's home and to find, instead, an apartment of her own.

Nandita's exhibition was reviewed in the newspaper on the page directly opposite the one on which appeared Father O'Leary's article for that day. Although Nandita was a Hindu, albeit non-practising, she usually read Father O'Leary's contributions. His articles were talked about by people of all persuasions, and she herself found them curiously compelling, as well as scandalous and humorous, whether he had intended them to be or not. But on the day her review appeared she had no interest, at least not immediately, in Father O'Leary and his ideas. The reviewer of her exhibition had been harsh, remarking that the hyper-realism possible—and even inherent—in the medium of photography, and as exploited by Sharma, was redundant and off-putting. Perhaps, the reviewer suggested, Sharma should make paintings from her photographs. The plasticity of paint combined with the physical, energetic act of applying paint to canvas would tame the subject, the reviewer predicted, and perhaps then the fruit of Sharma's excellent eye for composition and detail would adorn, as they should, walls of the homes of the island's art collectors.

This was Nandita's third exhibition at the gallery. In total, she had only ever sold two of her photographs through that gallery. She worried that the inevitable fallout of such a review would be no sales yet again, resulting in the gallery owner not wanting to invest in her in the future. Nandita had no doubt that she was an artist and that her photographs were art, but not wanting an I-told-you-so smugness levelled at her from her family, she needed to make her own living. She had never imagined the need to equip herself with any other skills. Even if she were able to do something else, the truth is, she had always felt that life would be pointless if she could not live it through the lens of her camera. The review devastated her. Furthermore, so public a denunciation of her medium sealed her reputation and fate, she feared, as a failed artist. She folded the newspaper in half, turned it over and left it on her kitchen table.

Later that day, sitting dejectedly with a coffee and a cigarette at the table, her eyes fell on Father O'Leary's article, titled, "An Urgent Need for Baptism Today." After some preamble about the origins and meaning of baptism, Father O'Leary managed to link the subject with his favourite topic—the jumbies that live in silk cotton trees. He wrote, "Silk cotton trees serve no purpose today, save as lair of the unbaptized and of their leader in the underworld, the jumbie . . . Before civilization, the Caribs and the Arawaks used to chop down silk cottons. They used the trunk of a single tree to carve out a whole canoe. But today, who needs canoes when we have airlines? In any case, even the fearless Caribs and Arawaks, were they still around, would not go near such a tree. For it is under those trees that the restless souls of people who have died without having been baptized gather. There are many such trees rather near to villages on the outskirts of the city, the one at Bonnaire being the closest and most accessible . . . Go close to those trees at night at your own risk. Seek com-

munion with those dark and restless spirits only if you are prepared to pay the severe penalty . . . All night long, in the vi-
cinity of silk cotton trees one hears a restless crying, a painful
wailing, begging and calling. Answer at your peril. They will
steal your soul and send you back to work for them among the
living . . . If you were not fortunate enough to have been baptized the day you were born, then get yourself baptized today."

That night, Nandita Sharma, her recklessness encour-
aged and fortified by the self-pitying consumption of one rum
punch too many, packed up a camera bag and a knapsack and
drove to Bonnaire.

Bonnaire, according to Father O'Leary, was off the Lady
Young Road, just east of the Hilton Hotel, and to the left of a
headless coconut tree in whose trunk was nailed a man's black
dress shoe. With such explicit directions for where one was
not supposed to go, and despite a number of quarrying trucks
parked on the rough shoulder, she found the road easily—even
with a bit of drink in her head. As she entered and immediately descended a steep hill, the lights of the city disappeared.
It was so dark that Nandita could not see her hands on the
steering wheel. She could see only what was caught in the
spray of light cast by her car's weak headlamps; the asphalt
road appeared to be narrow with deep tracks of dried mud.
Abruptly sobered, she reflected that she knew better than to
travel alone, day or night, in remote areas; her own father's
newspapers reported daily of murders, rapes, kidnappings and
robberies—crimes for which perpetrators were seldom caught,
and which, as a result, occurred these days with increasing
regularity. She drove slowly, contemplating the lack of wisdom
of what she was doing. She pressed on, not because she was
fearless, but because the worst of all fates, she decided, was
to have one's sense of self diminished by the ideals of others.

This was the crime, perpetrated all day long, every day, that she feared most.

According to Father O'Leary's article, one drove not far at all—just about a quarter of a mile in—until one found another headless coconut tree on which the shoe's other side was nailed, and one left one's car right there, where a footpath took one, through the high bush, to the silk cotton tree.

Closer to the road the footpath was easy to follow, but too soon it narrowed and was overgrown. On Nandita's back was a knapsack, and slung across her chest was the heavy camera bag. In her hand she carried a tripod. Thousands of cicadas chirped and whistled, and crapauds croaked like old dogs barking. Nandita tiptoed under the heavy snoring of howler monkeys. Her heart beat so fast it made her breathless. She stole through trees she knew by their smell—mostly guava, but there were lime trees too, and brush that clawed at her skin, cutting and stinging it. She moved as discreetly as she could, all the while listening for human voices and man-made sounds. Unseen creatures fluttered and rustled in the bushes, and several times something flew close enough that she felt a rush of breeze against her face as it passed. She stood still and tried to listen; the thunderous pulsing of blood against her temples was all she heard. She scanned the darkness for twin pinpoints of light that might alert her to the presence of a large animal or a human. It was a good thing she saw none, she thought, as the surprise and fright of it would have been enough to kill her.

She reached a clearing at the same time that the moon, which had been obscured all the while by heavy cloud cover, burst out and scattered a silver light. In the middle of the clearing was an imposing silk cotton whose enormous and pale grey trunk stretched up like an extended arm, at the end of which were branches spread as if its mass were a hand opened wide to the sky. Father O'Leary, short of giving advice, had written that people who went to the silk cotton to commune with the jumbies were obliged to wear patchouli essence because only patchouli could mask the stench of decay and evil that emanated from the base of the tree. Accordingly, Nandita had brought with her a phial of the scent and, without taking her eyes off the tree, she daubed herself with it.

Nandita stood still, only her eyes roaming, accustoming themselves quickly to the area. She held her breath, calmed herself and listened. There was an unusual stillness, as if time had stopped; the sounds she'd heard on the footpath—those of the cicadas, frogs, monkeys, night birds and insects—had ceased. The root system of the tree came slowly into focus, and a cave in one of the tall buttresses was revealed. Nandita had not budged and yet, with a blink of her eye, it seemed that she and the tree had moved closer to each other, and leaning against the entrance to the cave was the jumbie.

Wound raggedly around the jumbie's waist were sheets of burlap. He wore sandals, and about his neck was twined a thin shawl of some sort of dried and flaky material that Nandita couldn't identify. A long stick, a walking stick, lay across his lap. Nandita's teeth chattered in her head. The jumbie lit a match. As he navigated the flame to the pipe he held between his lips, the shawl around his neck hissed and crackled. The old man slapped his thigh and laughed.

He tugged at the shawl and said, "Skin! Relax! You done dry up. Can't dry you up no more, yet I can't shut you up. Shut up yourself or else I'll turn you back into a human, and then you'll see what misery is." The skin around the jumbie's neck chuntered like a peeved parrot, but finally gave up and settled down.

Nandita wanted to turn around and run, but the muscles in her legs had gone slack and there was a terrible tickling sensation running up and down her useless limbs. She cleared her throat, and was surprised and frightened to hear the sound come out of her.

Addressing the sound she'd made, a raspy high-pitched cackle came from the jumbie before he spat out, "You lose! I win! Couldn't wait, eh? I win!"

Had Nandita been blind, she thought, she would have assumed that the owner of such a voice was a crotchety old woman, but the barebacked person in front of her suggested otherwise.

"So, who send you?" asked the jumbie. "O'Leary? He only singing out how jumbie and duppy bad-bad, but he self is the best advertising we ever had. I can't keep up with how much people does come here, night after night, because they read his stories extolling our virtues!" Again he laughed out loud. "How you like that? Extolling our virtues!" The jumbie threw back his head of matted ropes of hair and sniffed the air. "Look here," he said. "How much time I tell that good-fuh-nutten priest that I don't like that patchouli scent he does tell all yuh to wear." She was about to apologize for the scent, but the jumbie carried on: "Listen! Listen. What you hear?"

Nandita listened. The skin was quiet, and there was still that deadly silence all around.

She shrugged and the jumbie said, "All you people with eye and ears in your head don't know how to listen. You have to listen with your whole body—in this case, with your feet."

Once presented with such an idea, she found that the possibility of listening with her feet was indeed imaginable, and she concentrated there, but still she heard nothing.

"We on this side," said the jumbie, "we living with the sound of quarrying all night long right across the Northern Range. Every day they come a little closer. Bulldozing all the trees and all the bush, all the flowers, all the nests, the homes of all the animals, and of all of we. For hundreds of years the people used to respect the silk cotton, but this generation think all the talk about the silk cotton, about jumbie and spirits, is chupidness. Well, enough is enough. O'Leary free advertising don't meant nutten if this forest disappear. Why he don't use his big words to educate people, to tell them that the forest disappearing right before they eyes. All you people ever ask yourself where we who does call the silk cotton home will go and live if the silk cotton chop down? Let me tell you a little secret: we don't disappear, we just move around. We will find somewhere else, that is certain, but town people might'n like where we will choose to set up, you hear? Anyway, never mind me. Is things so, I have on my mind. So, you! What business you have for me?"

Keeping her eye on the jumbie, Nandita stepped forward to put her offerings on the ground. She gasped. Something nearby must surely have died, for such a stink rose up. She covered her nose with one hand, thankful now for the patchouli, and with the other set down a pouch of tobacco, a bottle of Scotch, a bag of pennies, six red candles, two rolls of toilet paper and a bag of coarse salt. At this last, the skin hissed and wriggled violently about the neck of the jumbie, causing him to gasp and cough. He grabbed it, cursing unabashedly as he wrestled with it, until he had removed it completely. He scrunched it into a tight ball and dropped it to the floor not far from the bag of salt. It unravelled, and began to smoulder, as if it were about to catch afire. In a swift action the jumbie rushed forward, took a handful of salt from the paper bag and threw it on the skin, which immediately shrank, like burning cellophane.

"Dime a dozen, *oui*," he said dismissively, and then he turned his attention to Nandita. "I have to ask you again? Don't waste my time." As if he read her mind, he continued: "Yes, yes. Is true, I was once over on your end, and I carry with me such expressions. Don't waste my time. But over here, the truth, the whole truth and nothing but the truth—look, you see, another one—is that time is meaningless, open-ended, many-sided, a foolish concept from the fantasy world of all you living. That is why all you does die. Die, die, die. Because you bow down to this fantasy you call time. But who is you and what you troubling me for?"

Nandita noticed that while the jumbie seemed to be rather talkative, he was not into conversation. "I am Nandita," she said. "A photographer. That is what I came about." When the jumbie didn't respond, she added sharply, "I need to be able to make great, important, worthwhile photographs."

The jumbie steupsed and said, "God, all you people boring for so. You want to be famous. Well, who don't want to be famous?"

A rush of indignation flushed Nandita. She didn't like the position that she'd found herself in. She straightened, and before she could check herself, she snapped, "What makes you decide that I am like anyone else? You are not prepared to listen to me. I am a woman. I came here alone. I am vulnerable in your presence, expected to cower and supplicate before a spirit whose powers, let alone reputation and presence, are supposed to be awe-inspiring, if not terrifying. But you're bullying me." She was angry and, to her chagrin, crying now. She picked up her tripod and backed away.

"Boring and sensitive. How you will get along in that

world of yours, if you so sensitive? Stand up. Stand up to me!"
shouted the jumbie, stopping her from fleeing. More quietly
he said, "Boring, sensitive and definitely brave."

Nandita appreciated the part with the compliment. En-
couraged, she explained her situation: "It is either that I must
figure out how to take pictures that people, collectors, will
want to buy as art, or how to make people see that I am a
good artist and that my photography is art. Otherwise I will
end up taking illustrative pictures of pumpkins, or ripe tomatoes, or of politicians cutting ribbons, or of some councilman
watching a big hole in the road, or of a woman celebrating her
one hundredth birthday. Look, I just want those who see my
photos to stop and think, and to have their thinking changed
because of what they saw. And I want them to want to own
my work, to want to exhibit it in their homes and businesses.
I would not have come here if I didn't want something big.
Compared to what I want, fame is a small thing. I think I want
a change in society, more than in my own art."

"But you travelled here with your camera, didn't you? Did
you expect to photograph something here? Me, for instance?"
asked the jumbie, and Nandita realized that he and she were
actually conversing now.

"The truth is that I didn't really expect to see you. I intended to take a picture of the tree. The silk cotton tree, at
night, when people most fear it. I wanted to show that there
was nothing here, nothing to be afraid of."

The jumbie began to run his hand over his head and down
the front of his bare chest as if smoothing a shirt. "Well, sorry,
miss. I here. I promise I won't break the camera," he said, arranging himself on his bench, crossing his legs and posing with
his cigarette.

Nandita quickly unleashed her tripod and set her camera

on it. She was about to set up her flash, but the jumbie stopped her, telling her that a flash was useless under the circumstances.

The jumbie was quite the poser, sitting this way and that, unexpectedly patient as she fiddled with the settings on the camera and changed from one lens to another. After photographing the jumbie and the surroundings for more than forty minutes, she felt quite sure that she had made some outstanding photos, and began to dismantle her setup. She was easier now, pleased, imagining what the photographs would look like printed large and framed.

"Yes," said the jumbie, again as if he read her mind. "They will turn out pretty. Pretty and grand. People will pay you big money for these. O'Leary self will pay the biggest sum. In the thousands. Don't be shy with him. But of course, I as your model must be paid by you."

Nandita stopped her packing and looked at the jumbie.

"What? You thought I was doing this for free? Typical."

His use of the word *typical* maddened Nandita.

"What do you want from me?" she asked, feeling tricked.

"Ey! Drop the attitude, girl. You don't get what you want from a jumbie for free. There is always a price, and I am not talking about that tobacco and salt and candles and thing you bring there. When you take from the jumbie, you does get more than you ask for. You does get a little bit of his soul." The jumbie was about to say more, but he was interrupted by a shoo-shooing coming from the other side of one of the buttresses. He turned and shouted, "You can't see I busy? What you want, you old duppy?"

The voices grew urgent. Words were being exchanged, but they were garbled. The jumbie stood up and fumbled toward the wall. Nandita strained to see and hear but in vain.

The jumbie returned after some minutes. "But, eh-eh,

them duppy have they thinking caps on tonight, you hear!" he said. "Between them and me, we have assignment for you. Now listen to this. The pictures—sorry, photographs—you just take of me will only develop for you after you complete the task we have for you. Bargain?"

Slightly disheartened but eager to see the fruit of that little unexpected photo shoot, she agreed.

"You see all the killing in the country?" asked the jumbie. "People getting killed like flies. All this 'casual brutality'—to quote a famous writer—and nobody answering to any of it. The defenceless dead, the unfought-for dead, they restless for so. See here?" The jumbie held out his long stick and pointed it to the invisible duppies behind him and then swung his stick to indicate the area ahead of the tree, including where Nandita stood. "They all here right now. They ent going to have no peace until their killers are caught and brought to justice. What you doing same time so next Sunday night?"

"*Dimanche* gras," whispered Nandita. She couldn't mask the fear in her voice when she responded, "Same time so next Sunday night is just hours before J'ouvert."

"Wha? So you 'fraid!" answered the jumbie. "Look," he said, "is not us who ask you for something. Is you who ask. You want the assignment or not? How bad you want it?"

"I don't know if the streets will be open," she protested. She hadn't intended a long-term relationship with the jumbie. She hadn't intended much of anything, really, when she set out, except to take a few pictures of the tree at night. Had she really bound herself now, she wondered, to this other reality? "The police will block the roads," she said. "I don't know if I will be able to get out of Port of Spain."

"So now she 'fraid. She 'fraid, she 'fraid," he ridiculed. "Young lady, I thought you wanted this. Well, to get what you want, you have to want it real bad. How bad? This bad. That will determine if the streets will block up, if your car will work, if your camera battery will last, if a 32-megabyte flash card will turn by itself into a 208-megabyte flash card. You make up your mind. Yes? Or no?"

Nandita thought for some long moments. The jumbie waited. Her fear slowly dissolved as she recognized the potential for an opportunity of a lifetime. She answered in the affirmative.

The jumbie said, "We will make ourselves visible to all and sundry for that night only. Every person who get killed on this island since the beginning of the first injustice all the way to the present-day wantonness—from the native people in the days of the early Spaniards, to the slaves of the British, to the present-day victims of robberies and drug-related and poverty-related, greed-related and envy-, and jealousy-, and power-related crimes, all the people whose murderers weren't caught. All of us on whom justice turn its back. We coming, thousands strong, head bash in, eye poke out, neck break, vagina rip apart, heart blown up, brains hanging out, hand chop off, blood dripping-dripping fuh so. You think the dead don't bleed? Wait! You'll see! Displaced monkeys, birds, snakes, mosquitoes, crapauds and all kind of creatures will join us too, and will provide the music to which we will shuffle. People, not realizing till later that we are the real thing, will vote us band of the century. They will run from one street to the next looking for our band because word will spread fast about 'the band with the terrible yet amazing and mesmerizing costumes.' They will even want to drag behind us to the sounds of forgotten animals and the beat of our shuffling feet. They will think we are so creative!

"Every cell phone and small camera will be snapping-

snapping come J'ouvert morning, but next day, not one picture will actually have been captured. But we, the jumbies and duppies of Bonnaire, want to appoint you as the official photographer of our band. Is only you, and you alone, who will be able to take our pictures. See duppies drag theyselves on de streets of Port of Spain. See every Tom, Dick and Harriet snapping away with cell phone, video camera, pocket camera and expensive-fuh-so camera. See not one of them did capture a single image. Young lady here is the only one who could photograph the dead. And every face from the last decade will be recognized by the people who they left behind, including those who were responsible for their deaths, and those who have done nothing about all this crime. J'ouvert morning, the people of the island will have seen us come back from the dead. So, when they see your pictures, they will know that you didn't use them programs that does do fancy things with pictures, but they will know that you was special enough to actually capture them. You will be feared and respected, and your art will go international. Foreign will recognize you first, as usual, and then you will be on everybody A-list here. You ready for our assignment?"

The thrill of the prospects as outlined by the jumbie sent chills of excitement down Nandita's arms. "Where will I meet your band?" she asked, trying to appear nonchalant as she took a pen and paper from her knapsack to write down the directions.

The jumbie laughed. "You get yourself on the street, any street you want, and you will meet them."

Nandita returned to her car, breathless again, but this time with awe and excitement. She switched on the engine and the headlamps, glanced back to make doubly sure that her camera equipment was on the backseat where she had just put it, and, in an appreciative farewell gesture, turned toward the path that had taken her into the forest. But she couldn't see the path. She must have been rather disoriented, for even though she had just stepped off the path and into her car, the path was not where she had come from. Or where she thought she had come from. She looked again, farther up, then lower down. She was puzzled; it wasn't possible that she'd so quickly lost her bearings.

She unbuckled herself and leaned out the window. The moon had gone back behind the clouds, and the area was dark. That was it. It was too dark to see, she reasoned. She turned the car slowly and scanned the bushes lit by the headlamps. She repeated this manoeuvre, but now in the opposite direction. But the path had vanished. She drove on slowly, stopping every few seconds and leaning out the window to look toward the back of the car. Regardless of the distance she travelled as registered on the car's odometer, there was, she saw, no road behind her, only high bush. She was making a list of equipment she would need for J'ouvert morning just as her car reached the top of the road and met the Lady Young Highway.

ABOUT THE CONTRIBUTORS

MICHAEL ANTHONY is a Trinidadian writer of short stories, historical works, and novels. He was born in 1930 and moved to England in 1954 on the encouragement of Canute Thomas. He began writing short stories for the BBC and he also contributed to the Barbados literary magazine *BIM*. His first of thirty-four books was published in 1963, and his best-known novel, *Green Days by the River*, is being made into a motion picture.

ROBERT ANTONI is equal parts Trinbagonian, Bahamian, and US citizen. He is the author of five novels, his most recent being *As Flies to Whatless Boys*, which garnered a Guggenheim Fellowship and the OCM Bocas Prize for best book. His novels have been widely translated, and have been awarded the Commonwealth Writers' Prize and an NEA grant. He is the recipient of a NALIS Lifetime Literary Award by the Trinidad & Tobago National Library.

WAYNE BROWN (1944–2009) was a columnist, poet, editor, and teacher from Trinidad & Tobago. Widely known for his column In Our Time, which ran in Trinidadian, Jamaican, and Guyanese newspapers, Brown won the Commonwealth Prize for Poetry for his first collection of poems, *On the Coast*. He nurtured a generation of Jamaican writers through his workshops and an arts magazine which he edited for the *Jamaica Observer*.

WILLI CHEN is a Trinidadian-born Chinese writer whose work experiences include shopkeeper, baker, printer, artist, refinery operator, and entrepreneur. His art, poetry, sculpture, set design, plays, radio dramas, and short stories have won numerous international prizes. He still lives in Trinidad.

C.L.R. JAMES (1901–1989) was a journalist, socialist theorist, and writer. He was a founder of the Pan-African movement, cricket correspondent for the *Manchester Guardian*, and a prolific author. James's landmark works include the history *The Black Jacobins*, but he is also widely known for his writing on cricket, especially for the autobiographical *Beyond a Boundary*.

Arnaldo James

BARBARA JENKINS is a Trinidadian writer. In her late sixties, after a teaching career and the exodus of her children, she came to writing. Her short stories have won several international awards, appearing in *Pepperpot, Wasafiri, Small Axe,* and the *Caribbean Writer*. Her debut collection, *Sic Transit Wagon and Other Stories,* was awarded the 2015 Guyana Caribbean Prize for Literature. Her current hobbies are swimming in Macqueripe Bay's green-gold waters and visiting the ophthalmologist.

ISMITH KHAN (1925–2002) was born in Port of Spain, Trinidad. He attended the Queen's Royal College and went on to become a reporter for the *Trinidad Guardian*. In 1948, he left Trinidad for the United States, where he earned his master's degree from Johns Hopkins University. He taught at Medgar Evers College in New York for fifteen years. He wrote three published novels and a collection of short stories.

HAROLD SONNY LADOO (1945–1973) was born and grew up in Trinidad. He emigrated to Canada in 1968, where he published *No Pain Like This Body*. Shortly afterward, in 1973, Ladoo died an untimely and violent death on a visit home to Calcutta Settlement, Trinidad. He was twenty-eight. Ladoo's novel *Yesterdays* appeared posthumously in 1974.

Robyn Cross

EARL LOVELACE is an award-winning novelist, playwright, and short story writer. His many publications include the novels *The Dragon Can't Dance, Salt,* and *The Wine of Astonishment*. His latest novel, *Is Just a Movie* (2011), explores Trinidad's changing society in the aftermath of the black power movement in the 1970s. Since its publication, Lovelace has been awarded the Grand Prize for Caribbean Literature by the Regional Council of Guadeloupe and the OCM Bocas Prize for Caribbean Literature.

Michele Jorsling

SHARON MILLAR is a Trinidadian writer who has won the 2013 Commonwealth Short Story Prize and the 2012 Small Axe Short Fiction Award. Her debut collection, *The Whale House and Other Stories*, was short-listed for the 2016 fiction category of the OCM Bocas Prize for Caribbean Literature. She is a part-time lecturer at the University of the West Indies, St. Augustine, where she teaches prose fiction (creative writing).

SHANI MOOTOO was born in Ireland, and grew up in Trinidad. She is a visual artist, video maker, and fiction writer. Her novels include *Moving Forward Sideways Like a Crab*, long-listed for the Scotiabank Giller Prize, short-listed for the Lambda Literary Award; *Valmiki's Daughter*, long-listed for the Scotia Bank Giller Prize; *He Drown She in the Sea*, long-listed for the International IMPAC Dublin Literary Award; and *Cereus Blooms at Night*. Mootoo divides her time between Grenada and Canada.

V.S. NAIPAUL was born in Trinidad in 1932 and went to England on a scholarship in 1950. After four years at University College, Oxford, he began to write, and since then he has followed no other profession. He has published more than twenty books of fiction and nonfiction, including *A House for Mr. Biswas*, *A Bend in the River*, and *A Turn in the South*. He was awarded the Nobel Prize in Literature in 2001.

ELIZABETH NUNEZ is the Trinidadian-born author of nine novels and a memoir. Both *Boundaries* and *Anna In-Between* were *New York Times* Editors' Choices; and Bruised Hibiscus won an American Book Award. Nunez received the 2015 Hurston/Wright Legacy Award in nonfiction for *Not for Everyday Use* and a NALIS Lifetime Literary Award from the Trinidad & Tobago National Library. She is a Distinguished Professor at Hunter College, CUNY. *Even in Paradise* is her latest novel.

JENNIFER RAHIM is a widely published poet, fiction writer, and literary scholar. She worked for many years as a senior lecturer at the University of the West Indies, Trinidad. She edited and introduced two collections of literary and cultural essays with Barbara Lalla. Her poetry collection *Approaching Sabbaths* (2009) was awarded a Casa de las Américas Prize in 2010. *Ground Level: Poems* appeared in 2014. *Songster and Other Stories* (2007) is her first work of fiction.

ERIC ROACH (1915–1974) was born in Tobago, served for the South Caribbean forces in World War II, and worked in Trinidad as a teacher, public servant, and journalist. Though he devoted his later life to writing, producing many poems, plays, and short stories, his work was largely forgotten following his suicide in 1974. His collected poetry was eventually published as *The Flowering Rock* in 1992, cementing his legacy as a prescient and towering figure in Caribbean letters.

Eugene McConville

LAWRENCE SCOTT, a prize-winning author from Trinidad & Tobago, was awarded a NALIS Lifetime Literary Award by the National Library of Trinidad & Tobago. His most recent book is *Leaving by Plane Swimming Back Underwater*. His novels are: *Light Falling on Bamboo, Night Calypso, Aelred's Sin, Witchbroom,* and the collection of stories *Ballad for the New World*. He is the editor of *Golconda: Our Voices Our Lives.* For more information visit www.lawrencescott.co.uk.

SAMUEL SELVON (1923–1994) was a Trinidadian writer best known for his novels *The Lonely Londoners* (1956), groundbreaking for its use of Caribbean creole, and *Moses Ascending* (1975). He received two Guggenheim Fellowships and the 1969 Trinidad & Tobago Hummingbird Gold Medal for Literature. In 2012 he was named the recipient of the NALIS Lifetime Literary Award by the National Library of Trinidad & Tobago.

Danielle Devaux

DEREK WALCOTT is a Saint Lucian poet and playwright. He moved to Trinidad in 1953, where he cofounded the Trinidad Theatre Workshop. He received the 1992 Nobel Prize in Literature. He was also the recipient of a MacArthur Foundation Fellowship in 1981 and the Queen's Gold Medal for Poetry in 1988, among many other honors. His latest work, a book of poetry based on the art of Peter Doig, was published in 2016.

Naomi Howard

ELIZABETH WALCOTT-HACKSHAW was born in Trinidad and is a senior lecturer in French and Francophone literatures at the University of the West Indies. She is the author of a collection of short stories, *Four Taxis Facing North,* and the novel *Mrs B.* Her short stories have been widely anthologized and translated. She has also coedited several works, including *Border Crossings: A Trilingual Anthology of Caribbean Women Writers* and *Caribbean Research: Literature, Discourse and Culture.*

Permissions

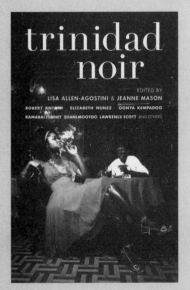